The Hateful Eight

Also by Quentin Tarantino

Django Unchained

Inglourious Basterds

Death Proof

Kill Bill: Volumes 1 & 2

Jackie Brown

From Dusk Till Dawn

Natural Born Killers

Pulp Fiction

True Romance

Reservoir Dogs

The Hateful Eight

Quentin Tarantino

GRAND CENTRAL
PUBLISHING

NEW YORK   BOSTON

Copyright © 2015 by Quentin Tarantino
All rights reserved. In accordance with the U.S. Copyright Act of 1976, the scanning, uploading, and electronic sharing of any part of this book without the permission of the publisher constitute unlawful piracy and theft of the author's intellectual property. If you would like to use material from the book (other than for review purposes), prior written permission must be obtained by contacting the publisher at permissions@hbgusa.com. Thank you for your support of the author's rights.

Grand Central Publishing
Hachette Book Group
1290 Avenue of the Americas
New York, NY 10104

www.HachetteBookGroup.com

Printed in the United States of America

RRD-C

First Edition: December 2015

Grand Central Publishing is a division of Hachette Book Group, Inc.
The Grand Central Publishing name and logo is a trademark of Hachette Book Group, Inc.

The publisher is not responsible for websites (or their content) that are not owned by the publisher.

Library of Congress data has been applied for.

ISBN 978-1-4555-3733-4 (Paperback ed.); ISBN 978-1-4555-3732-7 (Ebook ed.)

FOREWORD BY ELVIS MITCHELL

I think I was asked to write this foreword because I have a particular—and peculiar—relationship to "The Hateful 8." Partially because I'm lucky enough to be someone who gets to spend time with Quentin Tarantino, and those hangs can sometimes become an occasion where he'll suddenly dash off into a room at stately Tarantino Manor and emerge with a grin and a notebook, trailed by a flurry of loose pages: "So, I got this thing I was workin' on that I wanna try out on ya…" (He's up for sharing his writing with anyone he likes; a friend of mine got to enjoy this experience while seated next to Tarantino on a transatlantic plane ride.) And what he reads can be a chapter from a long-threatened treatise on a favorite director, or…OK, I know, this is completely unfair to bring stuff up that may never see the light of day (and which I mention in hopes of getting him to publish his unfinished books of film essays and director analyses). But—SPOILER ALERT, as they say on the worldwide net—this story has a happy ending. And almost no casualties.

Let's set the stage like this: Quentin Tarantino has taken a stab at almost any genre you can think of—often in the context of action film. And before you say, "Wait, not the musical…" I'd answer that with the dance scene in "Pulp Fiction," or for a more specific conflation, the Bride taking on the Crazy 88s in "Kill Bill, Vol. 1." (In fact, the similarity between musical and martial arts sequence is so easily limned—John Woo has basically made a career of it—that I'll leave that for someone else's intro, or graduate thesis.) Screwball comedy…really, do you have to ask? Romantic melodrama? "Kill Bill Vol. 2" is "Written on the Wind" as if staged by King Hu. Before we wear ourselves out here, I imagine there's one genre you'd be surprised to discover his interest in: the drawing room mystery. One of the first conversations we ever had included my embarrassed admission for a 1965 film, an approbation Tarantino shared. The film was "Ten Little Indians," which starred a Hugh O'Brian whose brow remained spectacularly unfurrowed as the plot ground inexorably towards a denouement in which a group of wan, guilt-ridden and overly tweeded swingin' Brits were eliminated as ruthlessly as comedies from NBC's prime time schedule. And it was Hugh's tanned superiority—even in black and white, he threw off a hearty Southern California glow (I think he even played a character named Hugh)—that led me to seek out the original source material.

Of course, you'd think Tarantino's attraction towards such a film would be about as likely as seeing a black person (a) starring in a premium cable series (b) starring in a Martin Scorsese movie or (c) alone on the cover of *Entertainment Weekly*. And those points of comparison come into play here for a reason. The 1965 film was an adaptation of an Agatha Christie novel called "Ten Little Niggers," complete with an equally glibly offensive song woven into the plot. And because Tarantino is one of the few working filmmakers eager to explore questions of race and identity in his work, the ugliness intrinsic to Christie's original conception was something he couldn't get out of his mind.

My contact with "Hateful 8" starts with its original incarnation; it was born as an intended print sequel to "Django Unchained," passages of which Quentin would enthusiastically read aloud from handwritten notebook pages, acting out every single action and character. Then, when it turned into "Hateful 8," I got to hear sections of that as well. When Tarantino asks for an opinion after he puts the writing down, the author-actor (**_acteur?_**) does more than listen for a response—he pores over body language and inflection from an audience as if he were Christie's Hercule Poirot, scanning the grounds in a demitasse cup for clues. Finally, the "8" script was finished and was on its way to production when it was leaked online. Now, that's a turn of events that demands its own Poirot, but the unhappy conclusion was that Quentin withdrew the material. It seemed it would never see the light of day.

And here's where what they call in TV shows the B-plot emerges. Film Independent at LACMA—where I'm curator—has a series called Live Read, where Jason Reitman and I put together a group of classic film scripts. Jason then casts them and for one night only, a group of actors reads the script before a live audience. (It's not streamed or recorded—if you're not there, you don't see it.) In the first season—we're now in the fifth—one of the biggest successes was a black recasting of "Reservoir Dogs" starring Laurence Fishburne, Cuba Gooding, Jr. and Terence Howard. It's the first—and to date—only production to receive a standing ovation after ten minutes in. In a reversing of the original casting, there'd instead be one white actor (in the movie, Holdaway, the detective who briefs Mr. Orange, is black). I asked Quentin to do it, and he was interested but too busy preparing the "Django" shoot.

While the smoke was still clearing from the explosion caused by the leak, I met Quentin for dinner. This was during Live Read's third season, and I'd invited guest directors since Jason was away making a movie. Earlier, I'd approached Quentin about being one of these special guests, but again, timing seemed to conspire against him getting to it. (I'm still hoping he brings the scripts he wanted to do to Live Read). So, I was caught off guard when he asked about stepping in as a guest director. I had to tell him the slots were all booked and there was no room left in our schedule. "What," he asked, "if I said I wanted to do a live read of 'Hateful 8'?" "I think we can make some room," I replied. Thanks to my agile staff at Film Independent, "The Hateful 8" had its world premiere April 19, 2014, on the stage at the theater at the Ace Hotel before a crowd of sixteen hundred people. What gets left out of this story when most people bring it up is that attendance was conditional. The entire audience had to check cell phones at the door for obvious reasons; Tarantino didn't want this staging turning up anywhere else, and Harvey Weinstein graciously paid for the extra security. And the place still sold out within an hour. That night, people from around the world watched as the writer-director cajoled, caressed and called-out a cast that included Samuel L. Jackson, Kurt Russell, Tim Roth, Michael Madsen, Walton Goggins, Bruce Dern and James Parks. If you're chewing your lower lip about having missed your opportunity to see them do it live, don't worry: they're all in the film version of "Hateful 8," joined by new arrivals Jennifer Jason Leigh, Demian Bichir and Channing Tatum. The period racism of Christie's novel becomes the foundation of this post–Civil War mystery, in which casual and blunt ugliness functions as a kind of original sin—something that stains every single character in the piece.

At the end of the "Hateful 8" Live Read evening—four a.m. the next day, actually—a handful of us remained. And as we smoked celebratory cigars, Quentin pulled me aside and confirmed a possibility he'd teased about—and which had to be kept on the d.l. between us—when he proposed the "Hateful 8" read: "This is it. I'm gonna do it. I'm making the movie." He broke into a reassuring chuckle, exhaled a plume of Cuban smoke and wandered back to the crowd, where he led them in a toast. The final chapter of that story that was years in the making is this, "The Hateful 8" script that—as Stan Lee used to write—you hold in your hot little hands, true believer. And me? As someone says in a movie by one of Mr. Tarantino's favorite directors, I just happened to be there when the wheel went 'round.

TABLE OF CONTENTS

Chapter One

Last Stage to Red Rock

CUT FROM BLACK TO:

70mm SUPERSCOPE WIDESHOT OF WYOMING

EXT—WHITE WINTER WYOMING MOUNTAIN RANGE—SNOWY DAY

A breathtaking 70MM filmed (as is the whole movie) snow covered mountain range.

A staggering opening vista, set to appropriately nerve jangling music.

Then, in the bottom left of this big 70MM SUPER CINEMASCOPE FRAME, we see a STAGECOACH being pulled by a team of SIX HORSES rip snorting through the bottom of the landscape.

Setting is an undetermined time, six or eight or twelve years after the Civil War.

                                                    CUT TO

EXT—STAGECOACH (MOVING)—SNOWY DAY

Now, still in big super CINEMASCOPE 70MM filmed gloriousness, we follow along with the lone STAGECOACH DRIVER fighting and guiding these six horses to shelter.

We follow alongside the HORSES, working our way from the back horse in mid-stride, to the tip of the lead horse's nose.

We follow along the twelve horse hooves as they tear up and spit out snow and dirt.

We take the DRIVER'S POV down the hurtling six horse team.

We follow along the big stagecoach WAGON WHEEL, then up to the stagecoach door WINDOW (complete with curtains). Which beyond we can make out the figures of a MAN and a WOMAN sitting side by side.

70MM CU of The STAGECOACH DRIVER O.B. (pronounced Obie) as he whips the horses forward, keeps the wheels on the road, and avoids the rocks.

Then . . . .

. . . . he sees something up ahead.

He pulls back on the reins.

CU HORSE MOUTH
as reins are pulled back.

Their HOOVES
slowing in the snow.

O.B.
still fighting the reins.

The HORSES
still trying to stop their vigorous glide. Snorting and coughing HOT BREATH, the horses finally settle to a stop.

O.B.
calms the halted horses, as he looks straight ahead and down at the impediment to his vehicle's progress.

O.B.'s POV:
What O.B. sees on the road is a BLACK MAN in the middle of it, sitting on a nice leather saddle, laid on top of THREE FROZEN DEAD WHITE MEN, smoking a pipe (the black man, not the three dead white guys).

The BLACK MAN
removes the pipe from his mouth and says to the man behind
the six snorting horses;

                    BLACK MAN
          Got room for one more?

O.B.
looks at the black man sitting on the three dead white men
in the middle of the road, smoking a pipe, amongst falling
snowflakes, and says;

                    O.B.
          Who the hell are you, and what happened
          to them?

The BLACK MAN is an older man. A sly LEE VAN CLEEF type
with a bald pate, silver hair on the sides, a distinguished
mustache, and a tall slim frame. He wears the dark blue
uniform pants of the U.S. CAVALRY, with the yellow stripe
down the side of the pant leg, tucked into black regulation
Cavalry riding boots. His shirt and undergarments are
non-regulation and worn for comfort, style, and warmth,
including a long charcoal grey wool scarf. But his dark
heavy winter coat is his OFFICER WINTER COAT from the U.S.
Cavalry, with the officer insignias ripped off.

On top of his bald pate he wears a supercool non-regulation
COWBOY HAT he picked up sometime after the war.

The NORTHERN OFFICER says;

                    MAJOR MARQUIS WARREN
          Name's Major Marquis Warren former U.S.
          Cavalry. Currently I'm a servant of the
          court.

The northern Officer stands up from his saddle perch on the
three frozen dead white men.

                    MAJOR MARQUIS WARREN (CON'T)
          These are a coupla' no-goods I'm
          bringin' into market. I got the
          paperwork on 'em in my pocket.

                    O.B.
          You takin' 'em into Red Rock?

                    MAJ.WARREN
          I figure that's where you goin', right?

We see a terrible BLIZZARD kicking up in the BACKGROUND. The
stagecoach has obviously been trying to beat it to shelter.

                    O.B.
That damnblasted blizzard's been on our
ass for the last three hours. Ain't no
way we gonna' make it all the way to
Red Rock 'fore it catches us.

                    MAJ.WARREN
So ya' hightailin' it halfway to
Minnie's Haberdashery?

                    O.B.
You know I am.

                    MAJ.WARREN
May I come aboard?

                    O.B.
Well smoke, it up to me, yes. But it
ain't up to me.

                    MAJ.WARREN
Who's it up to?

                    O.B.
Fella' in the wagon.

                    MAJ.WARREN
Fella' in the wagon not partial to
company?

                    O.B.
This ain't the regular line. The fella'
in the wagon paid for a private trip.
And I'm here to tell ya' he paid a
pretty penny for privacy. So if you
wanna' go to Minnie's with us.....you
gotta' talk to him.

                    MAJ.WARREN
Well I suppose I'll do that.

MAJOR MARQUIS WARREN starts to walk around to the
stagecoach door, when a rifle barrel comes out of the window
pointing at the former Cavalry Officer.

We hear a HAMMER CLICK.

The VOICE BEHIND THE RIFLE yells out;

                    VOICE BEHIND THE RIFLE (OS)
Hold it black fella'!

Marquis Warren stops.

                        VOICE BEHIND THE RIFLE (OS)
                        (CON'T)
            'Fore you approach, you take them two
            guns of yours and lay 'em on that rock
            over yonder. Then you raise both your
            hands way above your hat. Then you come
            forward. . . .molasses-like.

Maj.Warren looks up at O.B. and says;

                        MAJ.WARREN
                        (to O.B.)
            Real trustin' fella', huh?

                        O.B.
                        (to Maj.Warren)
            Not so much.

Maj.Warren walks over to the rock that the voice behind the
rifle chose as a good place for Marquis to relieve himself
of his weapons.

He places two revolvers hanging on his hip on said rock.

Then raising his hands above his hat, he slowly approaches
the stagecoach.

We see a bit of a face and a hat in the dark beyond the
window frame in the stagecoach door.

The voice behind the rifle snaps;

                        VOICE BEHIND THE RIFLE (OS)
            That's far enough!

The Major stops.

The rifle barrel is taken inside the window. . .

Then. . . .

. . . .the fella' in the wagon KICKS OPEN the stagecoach door
so Maj.Warren can see inside.

The FELLA' IN THE WAGON is a rough looking white man lawman
type, with a drop dead black hat and a walrus like mustache
above his top lip.

He one arms a rifle in Maj.Warren's direction.

The other arm is handcuffed to the wrist of. . . .

The FEMALE PASSENGER/PRISONER in the stagecoach with him.

She sits across from him, her wrist cuffed to his wrist, his
cuffed hand holding a pistol, the pistol pointed at her belly.

This once pretty WHITE LADY (maybe before the trip, maybe
years ago) wears a once pretty dress, and a once sexy smirk
under a man's heavy winter coat. Her face is a collection of
cuts, bruises, and scrapes. As if during this trip with The
Walrus Mustache Man. she took a few punches and falls.

The WALRUS MUSTACHE MAN says;

                    THE WALRUS MUSTACHE MAN
          Well I'll be dogged, you a black fella'
          I know. Col. Something Warren, right?

                    MAJ.WARREN
          Major Marquis Warren. I remember
          you too. We shared a steak dinner in
          Chattanooga once upon a time. You John
          Ruth, The Hangman.

                    JOHN RUTH
          That be me.
                    (beat)
          How long's that been?

                    MAJ.WARREN
          Since that steak? Eight months.

                    JOHN RUTH
          So why don't you explain to me what a
          African bounty hunter's doin' wandering
          'round in the snow in the middle of
          Wyoming?

                    MAJ.WARREN
          I'm tryin' to get a couple a bounty's to
          Red Rock.

                    JOHN RUTH
          So you still in business?

                    MAJ.WARREN
          You know I am.

                    JOHN RUTH
          What happened to your horse?

                    MAJ.WARREN
          Circumstances forced us to take the
          long way around. My horse couldn't
          make it.

                    JOHN RUTH
          You don't know nothin' about this filly
          here?

Motioning towards the woman with the barrel of his pistol.

                    MAJ.WARREN
          Nope.

                    JOHN RUTH
          Don't even know her name?

                    MAJ.WARREN
          Nope.

                    JOHN RUTH
          Well I guess that makes this one
          fortuitous wagon.

                    MAJ.WARREN
          I sure as hell hope so.

John Ruth makes the introductions;

                    JOHN RUTH
          Major Marquis Warren, this here is
          Daisy Domergue. Domergue, to you, this
          is Maj.Warren.

While keeping his hands raised, Maj.Warren touches the brim
of his hat and nods slightly in her direction.

DAISY DOMERGUE (pronounced DAHMER-GOO) gives Maj.Warren
an open handed wave with her free hand and says with a
smile;

                    DOMERGUE
          Howdy nigger!

That makes John Ruth chuckle and Maj.Warren frown.

                    JOHN RUTH
                (to Maj.Warren)
          She's a pepper, ain't she?
                (to Domergue)
          Now girl, don't you know darkee's don't
          like bein' called niggers no more. They
          find it offensive.

                    DOMERGUE
          I been called worse.

                    JOHN RUTH
          Now that I can believe.
                (to Maj.Warren)
          Heard of her?

                    MAJ.WARREN
          Should I?

                    JOHN RUTH
Well she ain't no John Wilkes Booth. But
maybe you might of heard tell 'bout the
price on her head.

                    MAJ.WARREN
How much?

                    JOHN RUTH
Ten thousand dollars.

                    MAJ.WARREN
Damn, what she do? Kill Lillie Langtry?

                    JOHN RUTH
Not quite. Now that ten thousand's
practically in my pocket. It's why I
ain't too anxious to be handin' out
RIDES. Especially to professionals open
for business.

                    MAJ.WARREN
Well I sure can appreciate that. Only I
ain't got no designs on 'er. One of my
fella's is worth four thousand, one's
worth three thousand, and one's worth
one. That's damn sure good enough for me.

                    JOHN RUTH
                    (meaning the three
                    dead white guys)
Who are them fellas?

                    MAJ.WARREN
Warren Vanders, Homer Van Hootin, and
Rebel Roy McCrackin.

                    JOHN RUTH
Let me see their paperwork. Like I
said, molasses-like.

Maj.Warren slowly removes the handbills from his winter coat
pocket.

John Ruth lowers his rifle from Maj.Warren's chest, and takes
the papers to study. He removes from his pocket a pair of
spindly gold framed reading glasses that he applies to his face.

O.B., up on his driver's seat perch, yells back at them;

                    O.B.
                    (yelling)
Look, I sure hate to interrupt y'all!
But we gotta' cold damn blizzard hot on
our ass we tryin' to beat to shelter!

                         JOHN RUTH
                       (yelling back)
              I realize that! Now shut your mouth and
              hold them damn horses while I think!

The grizzled guy studies the handbills.

Then raises both of his eyes and the brim of his hat to
study the black Major still standing with his hands raised.

John Ruth makes up his mind.

                         JOHN RUTH
              Okay boy, we'll give it a try. But you
              leave those pistols over yonder with
              the driver.

Daisy Domergue says;

                         DOMERGUE
              You ain't really gonna' let that nigger
              in here is ya'? I mean maybe up there
              with O.B., but not in here—

John Ruth takes the pistol in his cuffed hand, switches it
to his free hand, and brings the iron weapon down hard on
the side of Daisy's skull with a sickening CRACKING SOUND.
This knocks the woman onto the floor of the stagecoach on
her hands and knees. Blood trickles from her hair, and runs
down the side of her face.

John Ruth leans his big hulking frame over her on the
stagecoach floor, and says with real grit;

                         JOHN RUTH
              How you like the sound of them bells,
              bitch? Real pretty, ain't they? You open
              up your trashy mouth again, I'll knock
              out them front teeth for ya'. You got it?

From the floor, Domergue says;

                         DOMERGUE
              Yeah.

Yanking her cuffed wrist hard with his arm.

                         JOHN RUTH
              Let me hear you say: "I got it."

Domergue looks up at the brute with hate flashing in her
eyes, and says;

                    DOMERGUE
          I got it.

                    JOHN RUTH
          You damn well better.

After Ruth is through dealing with Domergue, he turns back
to face Maj.Warren.

                    MAJ.WARREN
          I'm gonna' need some help tyin' these
          fella's up on the roof.

                    JOHN RUTH
          Give O.B. fifty dollars when ya' get to
          Red Rock, and he'll help ya'.

                    MAJ.WARREN
          Well, I think O.B.'s right. That storm's
          got me kinda' concerned. We get goin' a
          lot faster you help too.

                    JOHN RUTH
                    (irritated)
          Goddamit to hell, I'm already regretting
          this! Now I can't likely help ya' tie
          fella's to the roof with my wrist cuffed
          to hers. And my wrist is gonna' stay
          cuffed to hers, and she ain't never
          gonna' leave my goddamn side, until I
          personally put her in the Red Rock jail!
          Now do you got that?

                    MAJ.WARREN
          Yeah, I got it.

Maj.Warren walks over to O.B. on his driver's perch.

                    MAJ.WARREN
          You help me tie these fellas up on the
          roof, I'll make it worth your while, we
          get to Red Rock.

                    O.B.
          I hear you makin' eight thousand off
          these dead fuckers?

                    MAJ.WARREN
          Yeah.

                    O.B.
I'll help ya' for two hundred and fifty
dollars.

                    MAJ.WARREN
How 'bout a hundred and fifty dollars,
and first two days we in Red Rock, I
pay for all your booze. They got 'em a
social club in Red Rock?

                    O.B.
Why yes they do.

                    MAJ.WARREN
I'll stake ya' a night there too.
Now that's a good deal, son.

O.B. lights up.

                    O.B.
Shit fire, that's a damn good deal!

He leaps to the ground, and shakes hands with the black Major.

                    O.B.
You gotta' deal, smoke. Let's get to it.

                                  TIME CUT

EXT—SNOW WHITE WYOMING MOUNTAIN ROAD—SNOWY DAY

SLOW MOTION EMPTY FRAME
We hear the slow motion sounds of the horses running and
grunting through cold. Then we see the noses of the two lead
horses bob into FRAME. Then with a little more effort on
their part, their faces.

SLOW MOTION HORSE HOOVES
tear and kick up the snow as they move forward.
We hear only the slow motion horse sounds.

INT—STAGECOACH (MOVING)—SNOWY DAY

MAJOR MARQUIS WARREN
sits on one side of the stagecoach, preparing his pipe for
smoking.

JOHN RUTH & DAISY DOMERGUE
attached at the wrists, sit beside each other on the opposite
side of the wagon.

John Ruth's pistol is pulled and sits on his lap. Barrel
lazily pointed in the direction of Domergue.......

.......or Maj.Warren....if need be.

JOHN RUTH
prepares his pipe for smoking as well.

> JOHN RUTH
> So what happened to your horse?

> MAJ.WARREN
> He was pretty old. I done had him for a
> bit. When the weather took a turn for
> the worse, he did what he could, but it
> got to be too much for 'em.

> JOHN RUTH
> That's too bad.

> MAJ.WARREN
> Yes it is. Me an' ole' Lash rode a lotta'
> miles together. You might say he was
> my best friend—if I considered stupid
> animals friends....which I don't.
> Never the less....I'm gonna' miss 'em.

John Ruth lights his pipe with a MATCH STROKE, and says;

> JOHN RUTH
> I had a horse like that once—bout twenty
> years ago. Called 'em Cauliflower. Use to
> call 'em my "beast friend".

> MAJ.WARREN
> What happened to him?

> JOHN RUTH
> Some rattlesnakes shot 'em out from
> under me.

> MAJ.WARREN
> Didja' make it right?

The black man touches the match flame to the tobacco in the
pipe bowl.

John Ruth PUFFS some SMOKE out of the side of his walrus
mustache;

> JOHN RUTH
> Oh, you know I did.

EXT—SNOW WHITE WYOMING MOUNTAIN ROAD—SNOWY DAY

OVERHEAD SHOT—SLOW MOTION
The six horse pulled stagecoach with three dead frozen men now tied to the roof rides through FRAME.

BACK TO THE STAGECOACH (MOVING)

MAJ.WARREN
says;

> MAJ.WARREN
> (to John Ruth)
> So who's Daisy Domergue?

> JOHN RUTH
> A no damn good murdering bitch, that's who.

> MAJ.WARREN
> How long you been haulin' her?

> JOHN RUTH
> Five days. Caught her tryin' to catch a boat to Italy.

> MAJ.WARREN
> What happened to her face?

> JOHN RUTH
> Disagreements.

> MAJ.WARREN
> I can see you ain't got mixed emotions 'bout bringing a woman to a rope.

> JOHN RUTH
> If by woman, you mean her?

Jerking a thumb in Domergue's direction.

> JOHN RUTH
> (CON'T)
> No I do not have mixed emotions.

> MAJ.WARREN
> So you takin' her into Red Rock to hang?

> JOHN RUTH
> You bet.

> MAJ.WARREN
> Gonna' wait to watch it?

                    JOHN RUTH
          You know I am. I wanna' hear her neck
          snap with my own two ears.

Domergue says wearily;

                    DOMERGUE
          Enjoy yourself John. If the shoe was on
          the other foot, I'd laugh as you died.

                    JOHN RUTH
          Now that I can believe.
                    (to Maj.Warren)
          You never wait to watch 'em hang?

                    MAJ.WARREN
          My bounties never hang, cause I never
          bring 'em in alive.

                    JOHN RUTH
          Never?

                    MAJ.WARREN
          Never ever. We talked about this in
          Chattanooga. Bringing desperate men
          in alive—is a good way to get yourself
          dead.

                    JOHN RUTH
          Can't catch me sleepin' if I don't close
          my eyes.

                    MAJ.WARREN
          Yeah well, I don't wanna' work that hard.

                    JOHN RUTH
          No one said the job was suppose to be easy.

                    MAJ.WARREN
          No one said it was suppose to be that
          hard, neither.
                    (to Domergue)
          But that, little lady, is why they call
          him "The Hangman". When the handbill
          says DEAD OR ALIVE, the rest of us
          shoot ya' in the back from up on top of
          a perch somewhere, bring ya' in dead
          over a saddle. But when John Ruth The
          Hangman catches ya', you don't die by
          a bullet in the back. When the Hangman
          catches you . . . you hang.

Domergue looks sideways at the black man across from her,
and says;

> DOMERGUE
> (to Maj.Warren)
> You overrate 'em nigger. I'll give
> you he got guts. But in the brains
> department, he like a man who took a
> high dive in a low well.

Domergue LAUGHS at her own joke....

SUDDENLY....

John Ruth ELBOWS Domergue HARD IN THE FACE.

She SCREAMS, as her hands go to her face.

John Ruth leans closer to her and says;

> JOHN RUTH
> Now Daisy, I want us to work out a
> signal system of communication. When I
> elbow you real hard in the face...that
> means shut up.

Daisy looks at Ruth, she couldn't hate him more.

> JOHN RUTH
> You got it?

> DOMERGUE
> I got it.

Major Warren LAUGHS.

Daisy's eyes flash across the wagon over to the black man.

She couldn't hate John Ruth more.

That is unless he was a laughing nigger.

Then in that case, maybe she could hate him more.

They ride along quiet for a bit, when John Ruth asks
Maj.Warren;

> JOHN RUTH
> (to Maj.Warren)
> I know we only met each other once
> before. And I don't mean to unduly
> imply intimacy. But-a......do you still
> got it?

Maj.Warren knowing perfectly well what the old dog is
referring to;

>   MAJ.WARREN
>   Do I still got, what?

>   JOHN RUTH
>   ...the Lincoln letter?

>   MAJ.WARREN
>   Of course.

>   JOHN RUTH
>   Do you got it on you?

Maj.Warren nods his hat brim, yes.

>   JOHN RUTH
>   Where?

Maj.Warren takes two fingers and points at his heart.

>   MAJ.WARREN
>   Right here.

>   JOHN RUTH
>   Look, I know you gotta' be real careful
>   with it and all. I can imagine you
>   probably don't want to take it in an'out
>   of the envelope all that often. But if
>   you wouldn't mind, I'd sure appreciate
>   seein' it again.

>   MAJ.WARREN
>   Well, like you said, I don't like taking
>   it in an'out of the envelope that often.
>   However seein' as you're saving my life
>   an' all, I suppose I could let you read
>   it again.

John Ruth breaks into a big grin.

Maj.Warren carefully takes out an envelope from his inside
jacket pocket.

John Ruth watches the envelope....

Maj.Warren ever so carefully removes the letter inside the
envelope.....

John Ruth puts on his spindly reading glasses.

....then carefully opens up the letter from its folded position...

...then hands the open letter to John Ruth.

Daisy Domergue has no idea what's up with this letter.

JOHN RUTH READS
the letter. Moving his lips along with the words, but not saying them out loud.

MAJ.WARREN WATCHES
him read.

John Ruth looks up from the letter, to Maj.Warren sitting across from him.

> JOHN RUTH
> (reading from
> the letter)
> "Ole' Mary Todd's callin', so I guess it
> must be time for bed"
> .....Ole' Mary Todd.....
> (to Maj.Warren)
> That gets me.

> MAJ.WARREN
> That gets me too.

John Ruth turns to Domergue, and holds out the letter in front of her.

> JOHN RUTH
> You know what this is, tramp? It's a
> letter from Lincoln. It's a letter from
> Lincoln to him.
> (pointing at
> Maj.Warren)
> They shared a correspondence during the
> war. They was pen pals. This is just one
> of the letters.

Daisy Domergue looks over at the letter with interest....

THEN....

HOCKS UP A LOOGIE
and SPITS it on the letter with a BIG SPLAT!

This shocks both Maj.Warren and John Ruth.

MAJ.WARREN SLAMS his FIST into the right side of DOMERGUE'S
FACE...so hard...he ends up punching her into the
stagecoach door with such force...IT FLIES OPEN...and
DOMERGUE TUMBLES OUT of the six horse pulled vehicle...the
handcuff chain taking JOHN RUTH WITH HER...as well as the
Lincoln letter...and John Ruth's rifle.

EXT—STAGECOACH ROAD—SNOWY DAY

Daisy Domergue and John Ruth go flying out of the speeding
wagon, tumbling and somersaulting in the snow.

O.B. pulls up on the reins yelling at the ponies, bringing
the fast steeds to a slushy stop.

John Ruth lies in the snow, still chained to the dazed
Domergue, holding his arm in pain.

                    JOHN RUTH
                    (cursing at
                    the cold)
          ...of all the stupid—like to rip my
          goddamn arm off!

Maj.Warren climbs out of the stopped vehicle.

John Ruth takes out a SMALL KEY, and for the first time in
the story, UNLOCKS the handcuffs that tie him to his female
prisoner.

For the moment...both John Ruth and Daisy Domergue are free.

He doesn't want to unchain Domergue, but his arm hurts like
the dickens, and he has to walk it off.

Daisy Domergue spits some blood from her mouth into the
snow. She touches her freed wrist. She watches John Ruth
walk off the pain in his shoulder. "Awww, he hurt his arm,
ain't that too bad", she thinks to herself.

Maj.Warren looks for his Lincoln letter.

John Ruth yells at the Union Officer;

                    JOHN RUTH
          I didn't drag her stinkin' ass up this
          goddamn mountain, just for you to break
          her neck on the outskirts of town!

                    MAJ.WARREN
          You the one handed her my goddamn
          letter. I didn't give it to her, I gave
          it to you!

                    JOHN RUTH
          Okay, it's both of our faults.

Maj.Warren gives him a look. Then goes back to looking for
his special presidential correspondence.

John Ruth's arm feels a little better. He picks up the fallen
rifle and approaches Domergue.

With bloody teeth Domergue looks up at Ruth and says;

                    DOMERGUE
          That nigger like to bust my jaw.

                    JOHN RUTH
          You ruin that letter of his, that
          nigger's gonna' stomp your ass to death.
          And when he do, I'm gonna' sit back on
          that wagon wheel watch and laugh.

Maj.Warren finds the letter.

It's worse for the wear, but still intact.

John Ruth calls to him;

                    JOHN RUTH
          How is it?

                    MAJ.WARREN
          She didn't help it none. But it's
          alright.

Maj.Warren puts the Lincoln letter back in its envelope, then
puts the envelope back in the pocket of his winter jacket.

Then the colored Union Officer scoops up a handful of snow,
and crafts a snowball. He looks at Domergue.

She looks at him.

                    DOMERGUE
          Is that the way niggers treat their
          ladies?

                    MAJ.WARREN
          You ain't no lady.

Maj.Warren throws the snowball in her face, and trods off.

John Ruth looks down at her.

                    JOHN RUTH
You're about one wise word from being
tied up on the roof with them other
fella's. Now pick your trash ass up, and
haul it back in that coach. Open your
mouth again, and I'll feed it a knuckle
sandwich.

O.B. the Stagecoach Driver, calls from OFF SCREEN;

                    O.B. (OS)
Hey Mister Ruth?

Answering without turning around;

                    JOHN RUTH
What?

                    O.B. (OS)
We got another fella' on foot, up here
on the road!

Turning towards O.B.

                    JOHN RUTH
What?

He turns back around and glares down at Domergue.

                    JOHN RUTH
Is that it Daisy? Is that the surprise
you got planned for me—cause I know you
gotta' surprise planned for me.

                    DOMERGUE
Maybe the surprise is I'm tired of
runnin'.

                    JOHN RUTH
You're facin' a rope tramp, ain't
nobody get tired of runnin' from that.

                    DOMERGUE
You might be surprised John.

                    JOHN RUTH
If you're countin' on surprisin' me
Daisy, don't count on it.

MAJ.WARREN & O.B.
look down the road at something. John Ruth, rifle in hand,
joins them.

POV:
way way down the snow covered road, a lone tiny figure of a
man waves a lantern, trying to get their attention.

>   JOHN RUTH
>   (to Maj.Warren)
>   Considering there's a blizzard goin'
>   on, whole lotta' fellas walkin' around,
>   wouldn't you say, Major?

The Major looks at Mr.Ruth.

>   MAJ.WARREN
>   Considering I'm one half of them
>   fellas.....yeah....seems to be a lot
>   of us.

John Ruth points down the road.

>   JOHN RUTH
>   You know that fella'?

>   MAJ.WARREN
>   I know me some people 'round here. I
>   spent a lotta' time on this mountain
>   hidin' out from bushwackers. So maybe
>   I know that fella', and maybe I don't.
>   But I wasn't expecting nobody.

>   JOHN RUTH
>   You weren't, aye?

>   MAJ.WARREN
>   No I weren't.

John Ruth lowers his rifle barrel till it's pointed at
Maj.Warren.

>   JOHN RUTH
>   This changes things, son.
>   Eight thousand dollars a lotta' money
>   for a nigger. But with a partner....
>   ....eighteen's a whole lot better.

>   MAJ.WARREN
>
>   I don't have a partner no more.

>   JOHN RUTH
>   So you say.

                    MAJ.WARREN
          Why don't you take a gander at those
          three frozen fuckers up there. You won't
          find no holes in their backs. Well, okay
          maybe not Rebel Roy McCrackin, him I did
          shoot in the back. But shitfire, he
          deserved it. He not only shot my partner,
          he tried to steal my horse.

John Ruth, keeping the barrel of his rifle pointed at
Maj.Warren's chest, takes a pair of HANDCUFFS off his belt,
and throws them in the snow at the former Cavalry Officer's
feet.

                    JOHN RUTH
                 (to Maj.Warren)
          Put them on.

                    MAJ.WARREN
          I ain't wearin' handcuffs.

                    JOHN RUTH
          You put those on or you stop worryin'
          about this whole thing, right now.

Maj.Warren gives Ruth "a look", then bends down and puts on
the handcuffs. As he does, he says;

                    MAJ.WARREN
          You really think I'm in cahoots wit'
          that fella'? Or her?

                    JOHN RUTH
          That's my problem boy, I don't know. And
          until I do, you in chains.

                                        CUT TO BLACK

Chapter Two

son of a gun

CUT FROM BLACK TO:

MEDIUM SHOT OF THE STRANGER ON THE ROAD
He faces O.B., the wagon, and the horses. Holding a lantern
as the wind whips around him, he's a rather untrustworthy
looking man in his early thirties with rotten teeth and an
admittedly FLY WINTER COAT. His COOL BLACK COWBOY HAT is
turned WHITE BY THE SNOW.

Cutting straight after that CHAPTER CARD to this 70mm MEDIUM
SHOT of a new character suggests this new character is a
real SON OF A GUN.

John Ruth's voice yells out from OFF SCREEN inside the
wagon;

                    JOHN RUTH'S VOICE (OS)
          Hand your weapons to the driver.

                    STRANGER ON THE ROAD
          Little jumpy, ain't you?

The Stranger's voice pegs this new character as a stranger
from The South.

                    JOHN RUTH'S VOICE (OS)
          Never mind the jokes, just do it.

                    STRANGER ON THE ROAD
          If you say so.

                    JOHN RUTH'S VOICE (OS)
          I do.

                                        CUT TO

INT—STAGECOACH (NOT MOVING)—DAY

John Ruth next to the window has his rifle out and pointed at The Stranger. Domergue sits next to him cuffed to his wrist. Maj.Warren sits across from him with hands cuffed in front of him on his lap.

                    STRANGER ON THE ROAD (OS)
          Okay, I done did it.

                    JOHN RUTH
          O.B.? Ya' got 'em?

                    O.B.'S VOICE (OS)
                    (yelling back)
          I got 'em!

                    JOHN RUTH
          Okay fella', keep holdin' that lantern
          with that one hand, and keep that other
          hand where I can see it. Walk around
          here where I can get a good look at
          cha'. Real slow like.

John Ruth gets a good gander at The Stranger.

                    JOHN RUTH
          I'll be a goddamn dog in the manger.
          That you Chris Mannix?

The Young Stranger, with his arm raised, holding the lantern with the wind whipping around him, says;

                    STRANGER ON THE ROAD
          I'm sorry friend, do we know each other?

                    JOHN RUTH
          Not quite.

Inside the coach, with the doors closed, Maj.Warren says to John Ruth;

                    MAJ.WARREN
          You know this fella'?

                    JOHN RUTH
                    (to Maj.Warren)
          Only by reputation.

EXT—STAGECOACH ROAD—DAY

> STRANGER ON THE ROAD
> Like I said friend, you got me at a bit
> of a disadvantage.

> JOHN RUTH
> Keepin' you at a disadvantage, is a
> advantage I intend to keep.

> STRANGER ON THE ROAD
> Whoever you are mister, you sure sound
> tough when you're talkin' to a desperate
> man knee deep in snow. But I don't want
> no trouble. I just wanna' ride. I'm
> freezin' to death.

INT—STAGECOACH (STILL)—DAY

> MAJ.WARREN
> (to John Ruth)
> Who is this joker?

> JOHN RUTH
> (to Maj.Warren)
> You heard of the rebel renegade Erskine
> Mannix?

> MAJ.WARREN
> Mannix's Marauders?

> JOHN RUTH
> (to Maj.Warren)
> That's them. The scourge of South
> Carolina, Mannix's Marauders. That's
> Erskine's youngest boy, Chris.
> (to Chris)
> What brings you in my path, Chris
> Mannix?

> CHRIS MANNIX
> Well Mr.Face, I was riding to Red Rock
> and my horse stepped in a gopher hole
> in the snow, fucked up his leg, an' had
> to put 'er down.

John Ruth gives Maj.Warren a sarcastic look.

> JOHN RUTH
> Seems like a mighty bad luck day for
> horses.

> CHRIS
> Seemed like a mighty bad luck day for
> me too.....till I saw your wagon.

                    JOHN RUTH
          You got business in Red Rock?

                    CHRIS
          Yes I do.

                    JOHN RUTH
          What?

Chris flashes an alligator grin.

                    CHRIS
          I'm the new sheriff.

John Ruth snorts.

                    JOHN RUTH
          Horseshit.

                    CHRIS
          'fraid not.

                    JOHN RUTH
          Where's your star?

                    CHRIS
          Well I ain't the sheriff <u>yet</u>. Once I get
          there they swear me in, but that ain't
          happened yet. And that's when you get
          the star.

                    JOHN RUTH
          You got anything that can back any of
          this up?

                    CHRIS
          Yeah. When we get to Red Rock.

                    JOHN RUTH
          Not even a telegram....you know, like
          when they hired ya'?

                    CHRIS
          I travel light.
                    (beat)
          And from the look of those three frozen
          fuckers up there,
                    (pointing at the
                    stagecoach roof)
          I figure you're a bounty hunter open
          for business. And I figure you're taking
          them three dead bodies into Red Rock to
          get paid?

Tilting his head in Domergue's direction.

> JOHN RUTH
> Three dead. One alive.

Chris and Daisy meet eyes.

> CHRIS
> Who's that?

> JOHN RUTH
> Daisy Domergue.

> CHRIS
> Who the fuck is Daisy Domergue?

> JOHN RUTH
> Not a goddamn thing to nobody, except
> me and the hangman.

Chris finally gets a good gander at the men inside the wagon.

> CHRIS
> Well I'll be double dogged damned.
> You're The Hangman, Bob Ruth.

> JOHN RUTH
> It's John.

And spotting Maj.Warren in there too.

> CHRIS
> And you...you're the nigger with the
> head....Major Marquis. My lord, is
> that really the real head of Major
> Marquis lookin' at me now?

> MAJ.WARREN
> I'm really me, and it's really my head.

> CHRIS
> Boy oh boy...there was a time...What's
> goin' on, you havin' a bounty hunters
> picnic?—Never mind—you takin' in them
> three and her to Red Rock to get paid,
> ain't ya'?

> JOHN RUTH
> Yeah.

> CHRIS
> Well the man in Red Rock suppose to
> pay ya' is me. The new sheriff. So if
> you wanna' get paid, you need to get me
> to Red Rock.

                    JOHN RUTH
Well excuse me for findin' it hard
to believe a town electin' you to do
anything except drop dead.

                    CHRIS
So I'm suppose to freeze, 'cause you
find something hard to believe?

INT—STAGECOACH (STILL)

John Ruth considers the choice.

                    JOHN RUTH
I suppose not.

The bounty hunter KICKS the stagecoach door open. He removes
the last set of handcuffs from off his belt, and tosses them
in the snow at Chris' feet.

                    JOHN RUTH (CON'T)
Put them on and come inside.

Chris Mannix bends down and picks up the handcuffs at his
feet.

He examines them in his hand.

Then he tosses them back inside the stagecoach, they land on
the wood floor with a LOUD THUMP.

                    CHRIS
    No.

                    JOHN RUTH
Then you'll freeze.

                    CHRIS
Then you'll hang.

                    JOHN RUTH
    How so?

                    CHRIS
            (to O.B.)
Driver! Could you come down here and
join us?

O.B. climbs down off his perch and joins the conversation.

                    CHRIS
            (to O.B.)
You heard me tell this fella' I'm the
new sheriff of Red Rock, right?

                         O.B.
        Yeah.

                         CHRIS
        Red Rock is my town now. And I'm gonna'
        enter my town, in bounty hunters
        chains? No sir! Sorry bushwackers, I
        ain't entering Red Rock that way.
                    (to O.B.)
        When you finally get to Red Rock, you're
        going to realize every goddamn thing I
        said was right. And I expect you, O.B.,
        to tell the townsfolk of Red Rock that
        John Ruth let their new sheriff freeze
        to death.
                    (to John Ruth)
        There ain't no bounty on my head,
        bushwacker. You let me die, that's
        murder.

Chris Mannix just said a mouthful. A mouthful John Ruth
chews in silence.

The bounty hunter other bounty hunters call The Hangman
makes up his mind. He turns to Maj.Warren.

                         JOHN RUTH
                    (to Maj.Warren)
        Hold out your hands.

John Ruth takes a TINY KEY out of his inside vest pocket,
and unlocks the black man's handcuffs.

Every time John Ruth takes out that key, Domergue clocks it.

                         JOHN RUTH
                    (to O.B.)
        O.B., give the Major back his iron.
                    (to the Major)
        One thing I know is this nigger-hatin'
        son of a gun ain't partnered up with
        you. I'll help you protect your eight
        thousand, you help me protect my ten,
        deal?

They shake hands.

                         CHRIS
        Ain't love grand. Y'all wanna' lie
        on the ground and make snow angels
        together?

                         JOHN RUTH
        O.B. I said, give the Major back his
        iron!

O.B. leans in the wagon and hands the Major his two pistols
back.

The black man puts one back in its holster, and the other he
rests lazy on his lap.

Chris Mannix enters the coach, and sits in the space next to
Maj.Warren.

Before he climbs back up on his perch, O.B. closes the
stagecoach door, and says to the passengers through the
window;

                    O.B.
          From here on end, no more stops, or ain't
          none of us gonna' make it to Minnie's.

O.B. disappears from the window, back up on his perch on the
driver's seat. He WHIPS the SIX HORSES TO LIFE, and the whole
wagon RUSHES AWAY!

INT—STAGECOACH (MOVING)—DAY

MAJOR MARQUIS WARREN & CHRIS MANNIX
sit side by side, across from JOHN RUTH & DOMERGUE.

Chris Mannix looks at the outdoors speeding by the little
window in the stagecoach door.

                    CHRIS
          Phew doggie! That was a close one!
          There were a few hours there...I
          didn't really know fer' sure.

He lets out a LOUD REBEL YELL!

                    CHRIS
                    (CON'T)
          Good god almighty, it's good to be
          alive! Tell ya' what, Bob—

                    JOHN RUTH
          —The name's John.

                    CHRIS
          —When we get to Red Rock, I'll buy you
          and Major Marquis there dinner and
          booze. My way of sayin' thanks.

                    JOHN RUTH
          I don't drink with rebel renegades, and
          I damn sure don't break bread with 'em.

                    CHRIS
          Well Mr.Ruth, you sound like you got a
          axe to grind against The Cause.

JOHN RUTH
The cause of a renegade army? A bunch
of losers gone loco, you bet I do. Ya'
wrapped yourselves up in the Rebel Flag
as an excuse to kill and steal.
(to Maj.Warren)
And this should interest you Warren,
imparticular emancipated blacks.

DOMERGUE
Sounds like my kinda' fella'.

Chris says to John Ruth;

CHRIS
Sounds to me you been readin' a lotta'
newspapers printed in Washington D.C.
(beat)
Anywho.....I'm just tryin' to let
y'all know how grateful I am. I was a
goner, and y'all saved me.

JOHN RUTH
You wanna' show me how grateful you
are....shut up.

Chris shuts up.

For a moment.

Then he turns to Maj.Warren and asks quietly;

CHRIS
(pointing at
John Ruth)
Does he know how famous you once was?

Major Warren answers him quietly;

MAJ.WARREN
I don't think so.

Chris looks over at Domergue.

CHRIS
(meaning Maj.Warren)
Do you know who he is?

DOMERGUE
Do I know about the thirty thousand
dollar reward the Confederacy put on
the head of Major Marquis? I had kin
at Wellenbeck. Yeah, I know about Major
Marquis and his head.

John Ruth looks to Maj.Warren.

Chris explains to John Ruth.

> **CHRIS**
> For hillbillies, the head of Major
> Marquis was a new farm, or a ranch, or a
> business. Or twelve good horses, the kind
> you could start a proper stable with. A
> herd of long horns and a prize bull.
> (to Maj.Warren)
> Them hillbillies went nigger head
> hunting but they never did get 'em the
> right nigger head, did they?

> **MAJ.WARREN**
> No they didn't. But it wasn't for lack
> of tryin'. Them peckawoods left their
> homes and their families, and came to
> this snowy mountain, lookin' for me and
> fortune. None of them found fortune.
> The ones ain't no one heard of no more,
> found me.

> **CHRIS**
> (to John Ruth)
> Now it didn't stay thirty thousand the
> length of the war. Once passions had
> cooled, it dropped down to eight then
> five.
> (to Maj.Warren)
> What was it at war's end?

> **MAJ.WARREN**
> At war's end? There was still a regiment
> of Alabama veterans offering eight
> hundred dollars.

> **CHRIS**
> But, I bet even when it was five, you
> had your share of country boys comin'
> to call?

> **MAJ.WARREN**
> You know I did.

> **JOHN RUTH**
> Why did they have a reward on you?

> **MAJ.WARREN**
> The Confederates took exception to
> my capacity for killing them. After I
> broke out of Wellenbeck, The South took
> my continued existence as a personal
> affront. So The Cause put a reward on
> my head.

                    JOHN RUTH
What's Wellenbeck?

                    CHRIS
You ain't never heard of Wellenbeck
prisoner of war camp, West Virginia?

                    JOHN RUTH
No Reb, I ain't never heard of it!
          (to Maj.Warren)
You bust out?

Maj.Warren nods his head, Yes.

                    CHRIS
Oh Maj.Marquis did more than bust out.
Maj.Marquis had a bright idea. So bright
you hafta' wonder why nobody never
thought about it before.
          (to Maj.Warren)
Tell John Ruth your bright idea.

                    MAJ.WARREN
Well the whole damn place was just made
of kindling.
          (beat)
So I burnt it down.

                    CHRIS
          (to John Ruth)
There was a rookie regiment spendin'
the overnight in the camp. Forty-seven
men . . . . . . burnt to a crisp. Southern
youth, farmer's sons, cream of the crop—

                    MAJ.WARREN
          (to Chris)
—And I say, "Let 'em burn". I'm suppose
to apologize for killin' Johnny Reb? You
fought the war to keep niggers in chains.
I fought the war to kill White Southern
Crackers. And that means kill 'em any way
I can. Shoot 'em. Burn 'em. Drown 'em. Drop
a big ole' rock on their head. Whatever it
takes to put White Southern Crackers in the
ground, that's what I joined the war to do,
and that's what I did.

                    CHRIS
          (to John Ruth)
To answer your question, John Ruth,
when Major Marquis burned forty-seven
men alive, for no more a reason than
to give a nigger a run for the trees,
that's when The South put a reward on
the head of Major Marquis.

                         MAJ.WARREN
                         (to Chris)
              And I made them trees, Mannix. And you
              best believe I didn't look back neither.
              Not till I passed The Northern Line.

                         CHRIS
                         (to Maj.Warren)
              But you had a surprise waitin' for you
              on The Northern Side, didn't ya'?
                         (to John Ruth)
              See once they started pullin' out all
              the burnt bodies at Wellenbeck, seems
              not all of them boys were Rebs.

ON THE SOUNDTRACK in the B.G. we hear the sounds of a RAGING
FIRE...then we hear the SCREAMS and CRIES of MEN and
HORSES burning alive underneath Chris' dialogue.

                         CHRIS
                         (to Maj.Warren)
              Burnt up some of your own boys, didn't
              ya' Major? How many burnt prisoners
              they end up findin'? Wasn't the final
              Yankee death count somethin' like
              thirty-seven?

The Fire and Screams FADE OUT.

                         MAJ.WARREN
              That's the thing about war Mannix,
              people die.

                         CHRIS
              Ahhhh, so ya' chalkin' it up to "War IS
              Hell', aye? Well admittedly that's a hard
              argument to argue with. But if memory
              serves, your side didn't look at it that way.
              I think they thought, thirty-seven white men
              for one nigger wasn't so hot a trade.

FLASH ON:

INT—MILITARY COURT MARSHALL—DAY

MAJOR MARQUIS WARREN stands at full attention in FULL DRESS
CAVALRY OFFICER UNIFORM inside a MILITARY COURT ROOM.

EIGHT OLD WHITE MEN CAVALRY OFFICERS sit along a long table
in judgment on Major Warren.

Though we can't hear what is being said, we see the MIDDLE
OLD WHITE MAN OFFICER angrily accuse Maj.Warren of, as far
as the old white men sitting around the table are concerned,
a horrible crime.

MAJOR WARREN
stands at attention showing no emotion at the accusations.

Chris' dialogue continues as VOICE OVER:

                    CHRIS (VO)
          I do believe they accused you of being
          a kill crazy nigger who only joined the
          war to kill white folks and the whole
          Blue and Grey of it all didn't really
          much matter to ya'.
                    (all said in
                    one breath)

FLASH ON:

EXT—CAVALRY FORT—DAY

MAJOR MARQUIS WARREN stands at full attention in the
courtyard of a Cavalry Fort in full officer uniform.

A WHOLE REGIMENT OF COLORED CAVALRY SOLDIERS stand in line
at attention on one side.

On the other side is a WHOLE REGIMENT OF WHITE CAVALRY
SOLDIERS who stand in a line at attention.

The Middle Old White Man Cavalry Officer RIPS the OFFICER
INSIGNIAS OFF of Maj.Warren's uniform. Including all the gold
buttons down his blue uniform jacket. The coat separates,
revealing his bare chest underneath.

INSERT
A big stick with a white rag tied around the end of it, is
dipped into a bucket of CANARY YELLOW PAINT. When the stick
is brought out, the white rag is WET and DRIPPING YELLOW.

The Yellow End of the Stick is brought down the middle of
the BACK of MAJ.WARREN'S BLUE CAVALRY UNIFORM COAT.

MAJOR WARREN
Stands ramrod still as The Yellow Stripe is DRAWN down his
back.

The BLACK SOLDIERS
stand in line and watch.

The WHITE SOLDIERS
stand in line and watch.

The WHITE OFFICERS
who sat in judgment around the table, stand in line and
watch.

A DRUMMER
PLAYS a military flutter on his lone drum, the only thing
that can be heard other than Chris' Voice Over;

                    CHRIS (VO)
          And that's why they drummed your black
          ass outta' the Cavalry with a yellow
          stripe down your back.
                    (beat)
          Isn't it Major?

BACK TO STAGECOACH

                    JOHN RUTH
          Horse shit. If he did all that, the
          Cavalry woulda' shot him.

                    CHRIS
                    (to John Ruth)
          I didn't say they could prove it.
                    (to Maj.Warren)
          But they sure did think it out loud,
          didn't they Major?
                    (to John Ruth)
          But Warren's war record was stellar,
          that's what saved his ass.
                    (to Maj.Warren)
          Killed yourself your share of redskins
          in your day, didn't cha' Black Major?
                    (to John Ruth)
          Cavalry tends to look kindly on that.

                    JOHN RUTH
          I'll tell ya' what the Cavalry didn't
          look kindly on. Mannix's Marauders
          that's what. And the fact that Erskine
          Mannix's boy would talk about anybody
          else's behavior during war time makes
          me wanna' horse laugh.

                    CHRIS
          What my daddy fought fer' was
          dignity in defeat, and against the
          unconditional surrender. We weren't
          foreign barbarians pounding on the
          city walls. We were your brothers. We
          deserved dignity in defeat.

[39]

                    MAJ.WARREN
                    (to Chris)
        How many nigger towns you sack in your
        fight for dignity in defeat?

                    CHRIS
        My fair share, Black Major. When niggers
        are scared, that's when white folks
        are safe. You ask the people in South
        Carolina they feel safe? Our niggers in
        niggertown walk soft.

Maj.Warren lifts the pistol sitting in his lap, COCKS BACK
the hammer, and places the end of the barrel against Chris'
temple.

                    MAJ.WARREN
        Now you gonna' talk that hateful nigger
        talk, you can ride up top with O.B.

                    CHRIS
        No no no, you got me talkin' politics
        I didn't wanna'. Like I said, I'm just
        happy to be alive. I think I'll just
        look out this winda' here at all this
        pretty scenery, and think about how
        lucky I am.

Chris turns from the Major, and looks out the window.

We see the white wonderland landscape of trees and rocks and
snowbanks go rolling by in GLORIOUS 70mm SUPERSCOPE.

                                        CUT TO BLACK

Chapter Three

MINNIE'S HABERDASHERY

CUT FROM BLACK TO:

SERGIO LEONE CU
JESUS FACE
An extreme close up of a HANDCARVED WOOD FACE OF JESUS CHRIST.

We start on Jesus' Face and SLOWLY ZOOM OUT...to reveal
a very old statue. It's a handcarved wood Jesus on a HAND
CHISELED STONE CROSS stuck in the snow. The statue looks
like it was there hundreds of years before the pilgrims. It's
as if The Vikings marched up a mountain in Wyoming, chiseled
a cross out of stone, carved a figure of the saviour out of
a log, planted it in the snow, then sailed back to Norway.
The aesthetics of the statue reveal a Slavic origin. The
Jesus figure with its skinny, pointy physique looks more
like a crucifixion of Eisenstein's Ivan The Terrible than
the hippy saviour of Catholicism.

But the number one thing the audience will notice about the
statue, is an entire snowbank has built up on the longways
section of the cross. As well as two snow piles. One, sitting
on top of the cross. And the other sitting on top of Jesus'
head.

O.B. and the six horse team come whizzing by kicking up dirt
and snow as it whooshes by the cross and the 70mm CAMERAS.

CUT TO

EXT—MINNIE'S HABERDASHERY—DAY

The six horse team stagecoach pulls up to the front of the
log built building that's known as "MINNIE'S HABERDASHERY".

On the outside, Minnie's just looked like a slightly bigger
than normal stagecoach stopover, parked halfway up a
mountain. That's because, despite local reputation, that's
what it is. If serving two bottles of Tequila, one bottle of
Mezcal, and one bottle of Brandy qualifies you as a bar, it's
a bar. If serving stew qualifies you as a restaurant, it's a
restaurant.

It sells a few hats, gloves, and snowshoes for the stagecoach
passengers. And supplies for the mountain folk. And it
receives special packages for people in Red Rock. Like say
when Carlos Robante (Pedro Gonzalez-Gonzalez) in 'Rio Bravo'
buys those red bloomers for his wife Consuela (Estelita
Rodriguez), but doesn't want everybody in town to know about
it. If he lived in Red Rock, he'd buy them through the mail,
have them sent to Minnie's, and when they arrived, Minnie
would get word to him, and he'd ride out there and pick them
up. Minnie's was also a good place to hole up during a storm.
This wasn't the first time a group of passengers from the
stage had to sit out the snow. Minnie and her partner Sweet
Dave also traded goods. In fact the only stuff in their
store of any interest is the stuff they acquired in trade.
If that makes them a trading goods store, then they're a
trading goods store.

Minnie's Haberdashery is a lot of things, but the one thing
it wasn't was a haberdashery.

O.B. brings the horses to a stop. He sees something.....

ANOTHER STAGECOACH, horses put away, off to the side.

O.B.'s first thought is, there's already people here. His
second thought is, that's strange.

He looks around.

The storm has gotten uglier....the wind more brutal.

He sees the outside of Minnie's, he looks at the barn, the
outhouse. The field of white snow surrounding it. It looks
like Minnie's, but it looks a little spooky. But this storm
is spooky, so O.B. chalks up his feelings to that.

And into this spooky storm A MAN in a big winter coat and
hat comes out of Minnie's front door, and walks towards the
stagecoach. Just as he gets closer the passengers inside
open the shades on the windows of the carriage door. The man
sees it's four passengers sitting inside.

This seems to startle him.

He shoots off to speak with O.B.

INT—STAGECOACH (STILL)—DAY

All four passengers saw the man's reaction.

                    CHRIS
          He didn't look that happy to see us.

John Ruth, staring at Minnie's building, says;

                    JOHN RUTH
          I think he's already got 'em some
          customers.

EXT—MINNIE'S HABERDASHERY—DAY

The Man in the winter coat moves over to O.B.'s perch on the
wagon.

                    MAN
               (speaking with a
               Spanish accent)
          What the hell's going on, we weren't
          expecting another stage tonight?

Referring to the other stagecoach.

                    O.B.
          I can see you already got another one
          up here.

                    MAN
          I just got through putting the horses
          away.

The storm is really getting going now. So much so people
have to yell to be heard.

                    O.B.
          This ain't the normal line. But we are
          stuck on the wrong side of a blizzard,
          so it looks like you're stuck with us.
          Are Minnie and Sweet Dave inside?

                    MAN
          They ain't here. I'm running the place
          while they're gone.

John Ruth steps out of the stagecoach into the cold, dragging
Domergue along with him.

>   JOHN RUTH
>   Where's Minnie and Sweet Dave?

>   O.B.
>   He says they ain't here. He's lookin'
>   after the place while they gone.

>   JOHN RUTH
>   (to O.B.)
>   They ain't here...
>   (to Man)
>   ...where are they?

>   MAN
>   They're visiting Minnie's mother.

>   JOHN RUTH
>   Her mother? Who are you?

>   MAN
>   I'm Bob.

>   JOHN RUTH
>   So you're lookin' after the place while
>   Minnie's away?

>   BOB
>   Si.

>   JOHN RUTH
>   Coffy in there?

>   BOB
>   Si.

>   JOHN RUTH
>   Well whoever you are, help O.B. with the
>   horses. Get 'em outta' this cold, before
>   the blizzard lands on our heads.

>   BOB
>   I just put those other horses away.
>   You need it done fast, you need to help.

>   JOHN RUTH
>   I got two of my best men on it.

He says as both Maj.Warren and Chris Mannix climb out of the
stagecoach.

                    JOHN RUTH
                    (to the
                    two men)
          Okay freeloaders, get to work.

John Ruth YANKS Domergue away towards the front door of
Minnie's, when suddenly his arm is YANKED BACK.

He looks down and sees Domergue has stopped and squatted in
the snow to take a pee.

She looks up at him.

                    DOMERGUE
          You'd let a horse piss, wouldn't ya'?

Okay, maybe she's got a point. He lets Domergue take her pee.

INT—MINNIE'S HABERDASHERY—DAY

We focus in on the front door of Minnie's Haberdashery, and
only the front door.

We hear John Ruth outside, trying to open the door, but it's
nailed shut.

Then we hear PEOPLE INSIDE THE ROOM YELL OFF SCREEN at the
door;

                    PEOPLE INSIDE (OS)
          Kick it open!

John Ruth KICKS OPEN THE FRONT DOOR—The WIND from outside
WHIPS INTO THE ROOM—John Ruth and Domergue step quickly
inside, Ruth SLAMS the door shut behind him—CUTTING OFF THE
WIND—only to see there's no door lock.

The People Inside yell at them;

                    PEOPLE INSIDE (OS)
          You have to nail it shut!

Both him and her look at them, "What"?

                    PEOPLE INSIDE (OS)
          There's hammer and nails by the door!

As they hold the door closed, they look down and see a
hammer and a can of nails.

So as Domergue holds the wind battered door closed, John
Ruth picks up the hammer, grabs some nails, and begins
pounding them into a piece of wood on the door.

He finishes and starts to put the hammer down, when The
People Inside yell at him;

                    PEOPLE INSIDE (OS)
         You need to do two pieces of wood!

Both John Ruth and Domergue give them a bit of "a look", but
then turn back to the door. He picks off the floor another
piece of wood, and hammers it into the door and the wall.

When he finishes, he lays down the hammer and says;

                    JOHN RUTH
         That door's a son of a gun. Who's the
         idiot who broke that, that Mexican
         fella'?

He turns from the door to see The People Inside.

It's THREE MEN:

ONE, a BLONDE ENGLISH MAN who wears a grey European cut
business suit, who stands up when he sees the man and woman
enter the room.

Speaking with an English Accent;

                BLONDE ENGLISH MAN
         Good heavens, a woman out in this white
         hell.
                (to Domergue)
         You must be frozen solid, poor thing.

The Blonde English Man is a bit of a fop. Not a gigantic fop,
just a bit of one.

TWO, an OLD MAN with a white beard, in an old Confederate
Officer Uniform.

RANK: GENERAL.

He sits by himself in a cozy chair by the fireplace complete
with ROARING FIRE. He doesn't look up when the man and woman
enter.

and

THREE, a lone COWBOY FELLA', in a cow puncher uniform, tan
pullover shirt and pants, and chocolate brown leather vest,
and cool but worn brown cowboy boots and hat. He sits by
himself at a table in the corner.

We also take in the inside of Minnie's Haberdashery. As has
been reported by Bob, sadly no Minnie. Even without meeting
Minnie, we feel her loss to this building. With Minnie's
big presence this place comes alive and is homey and warm.
Without her, it's a cold shack full of junk.

There's a kitchen area, that includes a pot belly stove.

Two comfy chairs sit in front of a fireplace with a big warm
fire crackling in it. In one of the cozy chairs sits the
Old General, in the other was the English Man before he stood
up.

Across from the kitchen area, on the other side of the room,
is a Bar Area. A Small Bar, with Three Bar Stools. And Four
Bottles of Booze. Two bottles of Tequila. One bottle of
Mezcal. One bottle of Brandy.

A few scattered small tables for one to four. The Cowboy
Fella' sits at one of those.

A Picnic Table in the middle of the room for community eating.

An Old Piano in the corner.

And A Big Iron Double Bed that sits amongst the goods in the
store. It's Minnie and Sweet Dave's bed.

John Ruth answers the English man;

                    JOHN RUTH
          Where's the coffy?

The English Man points in the direction of the pot belly
stove.

Ruth YANKS Domergue in the direction of the pot belly stove
and the coffy.

The People Inside see the handcuffs that attach the two.

As John Ruth crosses the room heading towards the kitchen
area, dragging Domergue along like a rag doll, he asks the
English Man;

                    JOHN RUTH
          Looks like Minnie's got 'er a full
          house. When did you fella's arrive?

                    ENGLISH MAN
          About forty minutes ago.

                    JOHN RUTH
                 (meaning the
                 Cowboy Fella')
          Is that your driver?

John Ruth finds the coffy pot on the stove.

                    ENGLISH MAN
          No, he's a passenger. The driver lit
          out. He said he was going to spend the
          blizzard shacked up with a friend.

> JOHN RUTH
> Lucky devil.

John Ruth goes looking for coffy cups. He sees a half plucked chicken, makes a face at it. He finds a coffy cup, and pours himself a hot cup of Minnie's coffy. John Ruth takes a DRINK of coffy....Then SPITS IT OUT...

> JOHN RUTH
> Jesus Christ, that's awful!

The Englishman laughs.

As does Domergue.

As does John Ruth as he takes the coffy pot and dumps out the brown junk in it.

> JOHN RUTH
> Christ almighty, what that Mexican
> fella' do, soak his ole' socks in the
> pot?

> ENGLISH MAN
> I think we all felt the same way,
> but were a little too polite to say
> something.

> DOMERGUE
> (referring to Ruth)
> He don't have that problem.

> JOHN RUTH
> Where's the coffy?

The English Man points at a bag.

> ENGLISH MAN
> There.

John Ruth makes a new pot of coffy, dragging Domergue with him. As he prepares the coffy, he asks the English Man;

> JOHN RUTH
> So all three of you on the way to Red
> Rock when the blizzard stopped ya', huh?

> ENGLISH MAN
> Yes, all three of us were on that
> stagecoach out there.

> JOHN RUTH
> Where's the well water?

The English Man points at a bucket.

                    ENGLISH MAN
            Right there.

John Ruth adds water to the coffy pot and puts it on the pot
belly stove to boil.

Then suddenly Domergue BLURTS OUT;

                    DOMERGUE
            The new Sheriff of Red Rock is
            traveling with us.

                    JOHN RUTH
            Sheriff of Red Rock, that'll be the
            day! If he's a goddamn sheriff, I'm a
            monkey's uncle.

                    DOMERGUE
            Good, then you can share bananas with
            your nigger friend in the stable.

                    ENGLISH MAN
                    (curious)
            So the new Sheriff of Red Rock is
            traveling with you?

                    JOHN RUTH
            He's lyin', he ain't sheriff of nothin'.
            He's a southern renegade. He's just
            talkin' his self outta' freezin' to
            death, is all.
                    (to Domergue)
            What the fuck I tell you 'bout talkin'?
            I will bust you in the mouth right in
            front of these people, I don't give a
            fuck!

The English Man watches the terse exchange between the man
and woman with a visible amount of distaste.

                    ENGLISH MAN
            You never said your name, sir.

                    JOHN RUTH
            John Ruth.

                    ENGLISH MAN
            Are you a lawman?

                    JOHN RUTH
            I'm takin' her to the law.

                    ENGLISH MAN
            So you're a bounty hunter?

                    JOHN RUTH
          That's right, Buster.

                    ENGLISH MAN
          Do you have a warrant?

John Ruth is surprised by that question.

                    JOHN RUTH
          'Course I do.

                    ENGLISH MAN
          May I see it?

                    JOHN RUTH
          Why?

                    ENGLISH MAN
          You're supposed to produce it upon
          request. How am I supposed to know
          you're not a villain, kidnapping
          this woman without a warrant in your
          possession?

                    JOHN RUTH
                    (irritated)
          What's your name, Buster?

                    ENGLISH MAN
          Well it certainly isn't Buster. It's
          Oswaldo Mobray.

                    JOHN RUTH
          Oswaldo?

                    OSWALDO
          Yes.

                    JOHN RUTH
          Well I got my warrant, Oswaldo.

John Ruth takes the warrant out of his winter coat, and
SLAPS it into Oswaldo's hand.

Oswaldo removes a glasses case from his suit coat pocket.
Out of the case he removes a pair of reading glasses, and
places them on his face. He examines the document.

He looks up from the paper to the face of Daisy Domergue.

                    OSWALDO
          I take it you're Daisy Domergue?

Domergue starts to say, yes—when John Ruth interrupts her.

                    JOHN RUTH
         —It's her.

Oswaldo goes back to examining the warrant.

                    OSWALDO
                  (as he reads)
         This warrant says, Dead or Alive?

                    JOHN RUTH
         Yes it does.

                    OSWALDO
         Transporting a desperate hostile prisoner
         like her sounds like hard work.
         Wouldn't transporting her be easier if
         she were dead?

As John Ruth puts the warrant back in the pocket of his
winter coat.

                    JOHN RUTH
         No one said the job was suppose to be
         easy.

                    OSWALDO
         Why is her hanging proper, so important
         to you?

                    JOHN RUTH
         Let's just say I don't like to cheat the
         hangman. He's gotta' make a living too.

Oswaldo Mobray reaches into the pocket of his suit vest, and
produces a BUSINESS CARD, which he extends to John Ruth.

                    OSWALDO
         I appreciate that. Allow me to properly
         introduce myself. I'm Oswaldo Mobray,
         The Hangman in these parts.

John Ruth looks at the card.

                    JOHN RUTH
         Well la-de-da.
                  (looks at
                  Oswaldo)
         Looks like I brought you a customer.

Oswaldo looks at Daisy.

                    OSWALDO
         So it would appear.

          DOMERGUE
Have you ever spent two days or more locked
up with one of your customers beforehand?

          OSWALDO
No I can't say I have.

          JOHN RUTH
          (to Oswaldo)
Don't talk to my prisoner. I talk to my
prisoner, that's it. You got it?

          OSWALDO
I got it. Jolly good.

EXT—MINNIE'S STABLE—SNOWY DAY

We see the four men left out in the cold, O.B., Maj.Warren,
Bob, and Chris, unhitch the six horses one at a time, walk
them across the snowy field to the stable, and lead them
into their stall.

All four men know how to handle horses.

The brutal wind gets more brutal still.

INT—MINNIE'S STABLE—DAY

The stable is a rather large affair. It houses eighteen
horses. Six from John Ruth's coach. Six from that other
coach out there that brought Oswaldo and his group. As well
as six other horses that would of replaced one of those
wagons if there hadn't been a blizzard.

It's quite a full house.

The four men get the six horses in to their stalls.

As they finish, Bob the Mexican says to the other three;

          BOB
I'll feed and water the horses. You go
inside and get some hot coffy. I've got
some stew cooking. Should be done soon.

O.B., who as an experienced stagecoach driver, has seen his
share of bad weather, says to the Mexican put in charge;

>   O.B.
> Look no matter how bad this blizzard
> gets, we still gotta' feed these horses
> and take a squat from time to time. So
> me an' Chris better lay out a line from
> the stable to the front door, and from
> the front door to the shithouse.

>   BOB
> Good idea.

O.B. and Chris grab some rope, hammers, spikes and get to
work on that.

After they leave, Maj.Warren says to Bob;

>   MAJ.WARREN
> I'll give ya' a hand.

>   BOB
> No don't worry, go inside, get warm.

>   MAJ.WARREN
> You're doing stable work in a goddamn
> blizzard, I offer to help and you say
> no?

>   BOB
> You're right mi amigo, muchas gracias.

The two get to the business of feeding and watering the
hard working horses.

EXT—MINNIE'S STABLE—DAY

Chris and O.B. stretch out a rope in the harsh snow and
wind.

One to the front door from the stable. The other from the
front door to the outhouse.

>   CUT TO

INT—MINNIE'S HABERDASHERY—DAY

John Ruth, with Domergue in tow, has relocated himself to
the makeshift bar drinking tequila out of clay cups with the
hangman Oswaldo Mobray.

                    OSWALDO
                 (to Domergue)
     Now you're wanted for murder. For the
     sake of my analogy, let's assume you did
     it.

John Ruth SNORTS.

Her eyeballs go to John Ruth for a beat, then move back to
Oswaldo.

                    DOMERGUE
     So....assuming that....?

                    OSWALDO
     John Ruth wants to take you back to
     Red Rock to stand trial for murder.
     And...IF....you're found guilty, the
     people of Red Rock will hang you in the
     town square. And as the hangman, I will
     perform the execution. And if all those
     things end up taking place, that's what
     civilized society calls JUSTICE.
                 (beat)
     However if the relatives and loved ones
     of the person you murdered were outside
     that door right now. And after busting
     down that door, they drug you out in
     the snow, and strung you up by the
     neck.........that would be FRONTIER
     JUSTICE.
     Now the good part about frontier
     justice is it's very thirst quenching.
     The bad part is it's apt to be Wrong as
     Right.

                    JOHN RUTH
                 (to Domergue)
     Not in your case. In your case, you'd
     have it comin'. But other people, maybe
     not so much.

                    OSWALDO
     But ultimately...what's the real
     difference between the two? The real
     difference is ME...The Hangman.
     To me, it doesn't matter what you
     did. When I hang you, I will get no
     satisfaction from your death. It's my
     job. I hang you in Red Rock, I go to the
     next town, I hang somebody else there.
     The man who pulls the lever that breaks
     your neck will be a dispassionate man.
     And that dispassion is the very essence
     of justice. For justice delivered
     WITHOUT dispassion, is always in danger
     of not being justice.

As the clay shooter leaves John Ruth's lips, he looks across the room suspiciously at The Cowboy Fella'.

The Cowboy Fella' sits at his table, writing in a little book. He BUSTS a peanut shell with his fist, then picks up the nut and pops it in his mouth.

John Ruth is just about to turn to Oswaldo and ask about the Cowboy Fella'.

When SUDDENLY we hear a LOUD SNAP SOUND, followed by the DEATH CRY of a surprised rodent. Domergue jumps.

                    DOMERGUE
          What's that?

                    OSWALDO
          Rat trap.

                    DOMERGUE
          What?

                    OSWALDO
          Rat trap. Minnie's basement is
          apparently filled with the filthy
          creatures. One less it would appear as
          of now.

John Ruth looks back over at the Cowboy Fella', he's writing in a book with a fancy ink pen of the day, which he dips into a blue ink bottle from time to time.

                    JOHN RUTH
                  (to Oswaldo)
          How 'bout that cowboy fella'? What's he
          writing in that book?

                    OSWALDO
          His diary, I suppose.

                    JOHN RUTH
          Well then it would appear the man has
          had an exciting life. What's his story?

                    OSWALDO
          I don't know, he doesn't say much.

                    JOHN RUTH
          What'd ya' mean, he doesn't say much?
          You rode up that whole hill together
          didn't ya'?

                    OSWALDO
          And he didn't say much.

                    JOHN RUTH
What's his name?

                    OSWALDO
I don't know.

                    JOHN RUTH
He never said his name?

                    OSWALDO
I don't think so.

John Ruth digs a SILVER DOLLAR out of his pocket. With his
thumb, he FLIPS IT THROUGH THE AIR, LANDING on The Cowboy
Fella's table with a LOUD THUMP.

The Cowboy Fella' looks up from his writing at John Ruth.

John Ruth dragging along Domergue, heads towards The Cowboy
Fella'.

                    JOHN RUTH
No offense cowboy fella', just gettin'
your attention.

The Cowboy Fella' lays his fancy pen down on the table,
leans back in his chair, and says to the bounty hunter his
first lines;

                    COWBOY FELLA'
You got it.

                    JOHN RUTH
What'cha writing friend?

                    COWBOY FELLA'
Only thing I'm qualified to write about.

                    JOHN RUTH
What's that?

                    COWBOY FELLA'
My life story.

                    JOHN RUTH
You're writing your life story?

                    COWBOY FELLA'
You bet I am.

                    JOHN RUTH
Am I in it?

                    COWBOY FELLA'
You just entered.

JOHN RUTH
Well you like writing stories so much,
why don't you tell me the story that
brings you here?

COWBOY FELLA'
Who's askin'?

JOHN RUTH
I am. John Ruth. I'm bringin' in this
one
          (gesturing to
          Domergue)
to Red Rock to hang. Ain't no way I'm
spendin' a coupla' nights under a roof
with somebody I don't know who they
are. And I don't know who you are. So
who are you?

COWBOY FELLA'
Joe Gage.

JOHN RUTH
What?

JOE GAGE
That's my name, Joe Gage.

JOHN RUTH
Okay Joe Gage, why you goin' to Red
Rock?

JOE GAGE
I ain't goin' to Red Rock.

JOHN RUTH
Where you goin'?

JOE GAGE
I'm goin' nine miles outside of Red
Rock.

JOHN RUTH
What's there?

JOE GAGE
My mother. I'm a cow puncher. I just
finished a big long drive. I wasn't just
an ass in a saddle this time, either.
I was partners on this one. For once
in my life I made a pretty penny. I was
coming here to spend Christmas with
mother.

                        JOHN RUTH
        Really?

                        JOE GAGE
        Really.

                        JOHN RUTH
        Funny, you don't look like the coming
        home for Christmas type.

                        JOE GAGE
        Well then looks are deceiving. Because
        I'm definitely the coming home for
        Christmas to spend with my Mother type.
        Christmas to spend with Mother? It's the
        greatest thing in the world.
                (beat)
        Is that good enough for you, John Ruth?

                        JOHN RUTH
        That's good enough for now.
                (beat)
        Steer clear of my prisoner.

He moves away from Joe Gage, and looks at the Old General.

The Old Timer, defiantly, doesn't look back.

                        JOHN RUTH
                    (to Old Timer)
        Hello old timer.

The Old Timer points out the General rank on his uniform.
Unlike Maj.Warren, the old timer's officer insignias haven't
been ripped off his uniform.

                        OLD TIMER
        General.

                        JOHN RUTH
                    (respectfully)
        General.

                        OLD TIMER
        You sir, are a Hyena.

Domergue laughs at this.

                        OLD TIMER
                    (CON'T)
        And I have no wish to speak to you.

John Ruth takes the insult for a moment, then says;

                    JOHN RUTH
          I've been called worse. Fair enough,
          General. Sorry to bother you.

Then we hear Chris and O.B. on the other side of the front
door.

EXT—MINNIE'S HABERDASHERY—DAY

Chris tries the door, it won't open.

Then he hears The People Inside YELL from the other side of
the door;

                    PEOPLE INSIDE (OS)
               Kick it open!

Chris and O.B. trade looks.

INT—MINNIE'S HABERDASHERY—DAY

Chris Mannix KICKS IN THE FRONT DOOR—The WIND from outside
WHIPS INTO THE ROOM—Chris Mannix and O.B. step quickly
inside, Mannix SLAMS the DOOR SHUT behind him—CUTTING OFF
THE WIND—Only to see there's no door lock.

                    PEOPLE INSIDE
               You hafta' nail it shut!

So as Chris holds the door closed against the brutal wind,
O.B. picks up the hammer, grabs some nails from the nail
can, and begins pounding them into a piece of wood on the
door. He finishes and starts to put the hammer down, when
the people inside yell at him;

                    PEOPLE INSIDE(OS)
               You need to do two pieces of wood!

Both O.B. and Chris give them a bit of "a look", but then
turn back to the door, and pound nails into another piece of
wood, sealing the door shut from the elements outside.

When O.B. finishes, he lays the hammer down and says;

                    O.B.
               Jesus Christ, that door's a whore!

Chris turns around and takes in the room and the people
inside the room.

> CHRIS
> Oh, I get it, haberdashery, that was a
> joke.

He sees John Ruth attached to Domergue at the bar.

And on the other side of the room he sees the pot belly
stove and the blue coffy pot on it.

The very cold Chris and O.B. head for the coffy pot.

> CHRIS
> (to John Ruth)
> How's the coffy?

Moving over to the pot belly stove, and where he goes so
goes Domergue, John Ruth says;

> JOHN RUTH
> Now, pretty good, if I do say so myself.

O.B. finds the cups.

Chris pours the coffy.

John Ruth and Domergue join them.

As does Oswaldo Mobray.

Chris and O.B. drink the coffy.

They both really like it.

> O.B.
> Damn that's good.

> JOHN RUTH
> Thank you.

Talking to Chris and O.B., John Ruth jerks his thumb in
Oswaldo's direction;

                    JOHN RUTH
          Guess who he is?

Chris takes a drink of coffy and guesses;

                    CHRIS
          Buffalo Bill?

The little English fop laughs at that;

                    OSWALDO
          Ha ha ha—hardly. I'm Oswaldo Mobray, I'm
          The—

John Ruth interrupts him.

                    JOHN RUTH
          —He's the hangman of Red Rock.

Both Chris and O.B.'s eyes raise.

                    CHRIS
          Oh, you are?

Oswaldo smiles at him.

                    OSWALDO
          Yes I am.

Chris offers his hand to shake, they do.

                    CHRIS
          Well good to meet you Mr.Mobray, I'm
          Chris Mannix the new sheriff in Red
          Rock.

Both Joe Gage and The Old General look up to see who's
talking.

John Ruth, chained to Domergue, says;

                    JOHN RUTH
                    (loudly)
          Horseshit!

Mr.Mannix and Mr.Mobray finish shaking hands, they both look
to rude Ruth.

                    CHRIS
          Pay no attention to him.

John Ruth continues with his boorish behavior;

                    JOHN RUTH
                    (loudly)
          HORSE-SHIT!

Chris continues with the introductions, despite John Ruth;

                    CHRIS
                    (to Oswaldo)
          Fella' next to me is a hellva' driver
          named O.B.

Oswaldo and O.B. shake hands.

                    JOHN RUTH
          That's the only thing you said that's
          the truth.

Chris ignores him.

                    CHRIS
                    (to Oswaldo)
          You comin' into Red Rock to hang Lance
          Lawson?

                    OSWALDO
          Precisely.

                    CHRIS
          Do you have your execution orders on
          you?

                    OSWALDO
          In my bag.

                    CHRIS
          May I see them?

                    OSWALDO
          Of course.

Even John Ruth would have to admit, if Chris is lying....he
sure is a convincing liar.

Oswaldo goes over to the BAG he left near the cozy chair
by the fireplace, next to The Old General. He opens it
searching for the papers.

John Ruth asks Chris;

> JOHN RUTH
> Who's Lance Lawson?

> CHRIS
> He's a fella' been sittin' in the Red
> Rock jail about a month now. He's the
> fella'—who shot the fella'—who was
> sheriff 'fore me.

Chris moves over by the fire, and takes the papers that
Oswaldo hands to him.

He reads them.

Everybody in the room watches him read the papers.

As he reads, Oswaldo asks him;

> OSWALDO
> What did she mean when she said, the
> bounty hunter's nigger friend in the
> stable?

> CHRIS
> (still reading)
> He's got a nigger bounty hunter friend
> in the stable.

> OSWALDO
> All that just to guard her?

Finishing with the papers;

> CHRIS
> I don't think that was the original
> idea, but that's the idea now.

He hands Oswaldo back his papers.

> OSWALDO
> So the new sheriff of Red Rock, and
> an African bounty hunter? Five of you?
> Well well well, looks like Minnie's
> Haberdashery is about to get cozy over
> the next few days.

> CHRIS
> Yes it does.

As Oswaldo puts away his papers, he asks Chris;

                    OSWALDO
          Are you the chap with the Lincoln
          letter?

                    CHRIS
          The Lincoln what?

                    OSWALDO
          The letter from Abraham Lincoln?

                    CHRIS
          President Abraham Lincoln?

                    OSWALDO
          Yes, weren't you pen pals?

                    CHRIS
          With the President?

                    OSWALDO
          I'm sorry, I heard somebody in your
          party had a letter from Abraham
          Lincoln, I assumed it was you.

                    CHRIS
          Well I ain't got no letter from Lincoln,
          and I can assure you, we weren't pen
          pals.

John Ruth INTERRUPTS and EXPLAINS;

                    JOHN RUTH
          Not him! The black fella' in the stable.

                    OSWALDO
          The nigger in the stable has a letter
          from Abraham Lincoln?

                    JOHN RUTH
          Yeah.

                    CHRIS
                 (to John Ruth)
          The nigger in the stable has a letter
          from Abraham Lincoln?

INT—MINNIE'S STABLE—DAY

Speaking of Maj.Warren, he and Bob The Mexican have
just finished feeding and watering the horses in the
stable.

> MAJ.WARREN
> What's your name?

> BOB
> Bob.

> MAJ.WARREN
> Warren.

They shake hands.

> MAJ.WARREN
> (CON'T)
> Minnie and Sweet Dave inside?

> BOB
> Minnie and Sweet Dave went to visit
> her mother on the north side of the
> mountain.

> MAJ.WARREN
> What, you tellin' me they ain't here?

> BOB
> Yes. They're visiting her mother.

> MAJ.WARREN
> Her mother? I didn't know Minnie had a
> mother.

> BOB
> Everybody's got a mother.

> MAJ.WARREN
> I suppose. And they left you in charge?

> BOB
> Si.

> MAJ.WARREN
> That sure don't sound like Minnie.

> BOB
> Are you callin' me a liar?

> MAJ.WARREN
> Not yet I ain't. But it sure do sound
> peculiar.

                    BOB
What sounds peculiar?

                    MAJ.WARREN
Well for one, Minnie just never struck
me as the sentimental type.
And two, I can't imagine Sweet Dave
liftin' his fat ass outta' his chair
long enough to fetch well water, unless
Minnie was layin' a fryin' pan upside
his head. No less takin' trips to the
north side.

                    BOB
That sounds a whole lot like you're
calling me a liar, mi negro amigo.

                    MAJ.WARREN
It does sound a whole lot like it. But
I still ain't done it yet. Minnie still
serve food?

                    BOB
Do you consider stew food?

                    MAJ.WARREN
Yes.

                    BOB
Then we serve food.

                    MAJ.WARREN
Minnie still stink up the place with
her "Old Quail" pipe tobacco?

                    BOB
Minnie doesn't smoke a pipe. She rolls
her own. "Red Apple Tobacco".
But mi negro amigo...I think you
already know this?

                    MAJ.WARREN
Just seein' if you do, Senor Bob.

The stand off is over. They both open the stable door, and
brave the brutal elements to get inside Minnie's with the
others.

INT—MINNIE'S HABERDASHERY—DAY

MEDIUM SHOT OF CHRIS
looking at something that's surprising him.

>   CHRIS
>   Well cut my legs off and call me
>   Shorty...
>   ....is that Gen.Sanford Smithers I see?

The Old General looks up from his chair at the young
Southerner.

Chris smiles at him.

The Old Man smiles back.

>   GEN.SMITHERS
>   You've got a good eye son.

Chris lets out a laugh and a twirl;

>   CHRIS
>   I'll be double dogged damned!
>   General Sandy "Don't Give A Damn"
>   Smithers!

Chris salutes the Old General.

>   CHRIS
>   (CON'T)
>   Cap't. Chris Mannix, Mannix Marauders.

Gen.Smithers returns the salute.

>   GEN.SMITHERS
>   Erskine's boy?

>   CHRIS
>   Yes sir.

Chris points to the empty cozy chair covered in animal
skins, across from The Old General.

>   CHRIS
>   (CON'T)
>   May I sit down, sir?

Instead of cordially inviting the young respectful man to
sit down, the Old Man says curtly;

>   GEN.SMITHERS
>   According to the Yankees, it's a free
>   country. Do what you want.

That wasn't quite a yes, but Chris decides to ignore it. I
mean his nickname is "Don't Give A Damn". So Chris sits down
anyway.

> CHRIS
> Boy did my daddy talk about you. I
> heard you gave those Blue Bellies sweet
> hell.

> GEN.SMITHERS
> Me and my boys did our part. As did
> Erskine and his boys. I never knew
> your father, son. But, I respected his
> resolve.

> CHRIS
> Thank you for saying that, General.
> Your respect woulda' meant the world to
> him. Can I getcha' some coffy?

> GEN.SMITHERS
> That would be nice.

Chris stands up from the chair, heads over to the pot
belly stove, and pours two cups of coffy from the blue
coffy pot. As he pours he talks across the room at the
Old Man;

> CHRIS
> So what bring you out Wyoming way, sir?
> If ya' don't mind me askin'?

The Old General never moves from his chair.

> GEN.SMITHERS
> My boy.

> CHRIS
> You gotta' boy lives in Red Rock?

Chris comes back carrying two cups of coffy.

He places one on the table next to the General.

As he sips the other, he sits down on the cozy chair covered
in animal skins.

> GEN.SMITHERS
> My son, Chester Charles Smithers, died
> out here a few years back.

> CHRIS
> Forgive me sir.

> GEN.SMITHERS
> No forgiveness needed. Like I said, it
> was a few years back. It was after he
> served his service. He took off for the
> hills of Wyoming to make his fortune.
> Never to be heard from again.
>   (more)

                    GEN.SMITHERS
                    (CON'T)
I've bought him a symbolic plot in the
Red Rock cemetery. I'm here to instruct
the stone maker of the headstone.

                    CHRIS
Is he a goner fer' sure? No chance he
could be livin' "the cold life" out in
the woods? It's a rough life. But folks
can learn it.

                    GEN.SMITHERS
If he had done what he came to do, he'd
a come home.

                    CHRIS
Where's home?

                    GEN.SMITHERS
Georgia.

                    CHRIS
Well what say we have a drink to
Chester Charles Smithers? A drink to
your service to The South, sir. And a
drink to the great state of Georgia.

                    GEN.SMITHERS
I'd like a drink from Erskine Mannix's
boy to my boy.

                    CHRIS
And that's a drink I'd like to drink.

Chris stands up, walks over to Joe Gage's table, borrows
the Brandy bottle, and snags two empty coffy cups. Returning
to the table in front of the Old General, he pours the
Brandy into the two cups. And while still standing, he picks
up one of the cups and raises it high to toast the sitting
General.

                    CHRIS
This is a drink to Chester Charles
Smithers. This is a drink to one man's
commitment to a cause. And this is to
the red in Georgia clay.

The Southern General and Captain drink the Brandy.

                    CHRIS
General Sandy Smithers. It's a small
damn world.

JOHN RUTH & DOMERGUE
sitting at the bar. He hears Chris say that, and leans over to
Domergue and says quietly;

> JOHN RUTH
> I don't know about the world. But this
> goddamn mountain sure seems pretty
> fuckin' small.

THEN . . . . .

BOB KICKS IN THE FRONT DOOR—The WIND from outside WHIPS INTO
THE ROOM—Bob and Maj.Warren step quickly inside, Bob SLAMS
the DOOR SHUT behind him—CUTTING OFF THE WIND—Bob says to
the Major;

> BOB
> You have to hold it closed, while I nail
> it shut.

> MAJ.WARREN
> Really? Who's the idiot who broke the
> damn door?

> BOB
> Just hold it closed.

Maj.Warren gives him one of "his looks" then turns towards
the door, holding it as Bob pounds nails into two pieces of
wood holding the door closed.

As the Mexican hammers the nails into wood, Maj.Warren
turns around and gets his first good look at the People
Inside.

Like O.B. and to some degree John Ruth, Maj.Warren
has been here before. But he's never been here WITHOUT
Minnie and Sweet Dave. And to see the familiar place
filled with unfamiliar people makes the Major uneasy.

As Maj.Warren removes his hat, he notices Joe Gage and
Oswaldo still wearing theirs.

When he finishes, Bob puts down the hammer, as Maj.Warren
turns to him;

> MAJ.WARREN
> A lotta' hats, Senor Bob?

> BOB
> Huh?

                    MAJ.WARREN
          Considering Minnie's no hats indoors
          policy? If I remember it correctly,
          that was one of them BAR OF IRON rules.
          Kinda rule, I'd think, she'd want kept
          up in her absence. But you seem to have
          a laissez faire attitude when it comes
          to the hats.

Bob turns to the sass mouth black Major;

                    BOB
          I'm guilty. I have a laissez faire
          attitude about the hats. How about
          we forget about the hats today,
          considering there's a blizzard going
          on and all, and make tomorrow "No Hat
          Day"?

Bob makes his quip and F.O.'s (fucks off). Major Warren looks
at the People Inside.

John Ruth and Domergue sitting at the bar with an official
looking blonde fellow in a grey business suit.

Chris sitting in a nice chair by the fireplace, with an Old
Man in a Grey Confederate Officer Uniform.

And a lone cow poke sitting by himself at a table.

He sees O.B. sitting at the picnic table. Maj.Warren goes
over to the pot belly stove, picks up the blue coffy pot and
pours himself a cup. He then sits down across from O.B. at
the picnic table.

                    MAJ.WARREN
          O.B.....? I gotta' proposition for ya'.

                    O.B.
          Well what do you propose?

                    MAJ.WARREN
          You asked for two hundred and fifty
          dollars the first time, right?

                    O.B.
          Yeah.

                    MAJ.WARREN
          How 'bout three hundred and fifty?

                    O.B.
How 'bout it?

                    MAJ.WARREN
You help me take them three fella's down
from off the roof, stash 'em in snow,
and when the snow melts, help me tie 'em
back on?

                    O.B.
And same deal about the booze and the
bitches in Red Rock?

                    MAJ.WARREN
Same deal.

                    O.B.
You gotta' deal Smoke.

They shake hands.

As the two men prepare to go outside, Gen.Smithers sits in
his chair looking at Maj.Warren with bitterness.

Chris Mannix notices it.

                    CHRIS
You know that nigger, sir?

                    GEN.SMITHERS
I don't know that nigger. I know he's a
nigger. That's all I need to know.

Chris laughs to himself.

                    CHRIS
Well that nigger just ain't any nigger.
That nigger is—

Just as Chris Mannix was going to name Major Marquis Warren
to the Old Man, Major Marquis Warren YELLS out across the
room;

                    MAJ.WARREN
General Sanford Smithers?

This gets everybody's attention.

                    MAJ.WARREN
                    (CON'T)
Battle of Baton Rouge?

Everybody looks from Maj.Warren to the old man.

The Old General never looks in the direction of the black
Major.

But he addresses Chris sitting across from him.

> GEN.SMITHERS
> Inform this nigger in the Cavalry
> uniform, I had a division of
> Confederates under my command in Baton
> Rouge.

> CHRIS
> Major Nigger, General Smithers wishes
> me to inform you—

> MAJ.WARREN
> —I heard 'em hillbilly.

> MAJ.WARREN
> (to CHRIS)
> Inform this old cracker I was in Baton
> Rouge as well.
> (beat)
> On the other side.

> CHRIS
> (to Maj.Warren)
> Oh that's interesting.
> (to the General)
> General Smithers, he said—

> GEN.SMITHERS
> Cap't. Mannix, inform this nigger I don't
> acknowledge the uniforms of Northern
> niggers.

> MAJ.WARREN
> You captured a whole Colored Command
> that day. But no Colored Troopers ever
> made it to a camp, did they?

The Old Man finally turns and looks at the black Major.

> GEN.SMITHERS
> (to Maj.Warren)
> We had neither the time, the food, or
> the inclination to care for Northern
> horses or Northern niggers.
> (beat)
> So we shot them where they stood.

Just as Maj.Warren's hand moves to his pistol butt, Oswaldo
Mobray appears between the two men and says;

                        OSWALDO
          Gentlemen, I know Americans aren't
          apt to let a little thing like an
          unconditional surrender get in the way
          of a good war. But I strongly suggest
          we don't restage The Battle of Baton
          Rouge during a blizzard in Minnie's
          Haberdashery.

Oswaldo does have a calming influence on the tension.

He continues;

                        OSWALDO
                   (to Maj.Warren)
          Now my Nubian friend, while I realize
          passions are high, that was a while ago.
          And if you shoot this unarmed old man
                   (placing his hand on
                   Smithers' shoulder)
          I guarantee I will hang you by the neck
          until you are dead, once we arrive in
          Red Rock.

Chris Mannix looks over at Maj.Warren and says;

                        CHRIS
          I guarantee that too.

John Ruth chimes in over by the bar drinking with Domergue.

                        JOHN RUTH
          Yeah Warren, that the problem with old
          men. You can kick 'em down the stairs
          and say it's an accident, but ya' can't
          just shoot 'em.

                        OSWALDO
          Now gentlemen, since we may be trapped
          here close together like for a few days,
          may I suggest a possible solution? We
          divide Minnie's in half. The Northern
          side and The Southern side. With the
          dinner table operating as neutral
          territory. We could say the fireplace
          side of the room acts as a symbolic
          representative of Georgia. While the
          bar represents . . . .
                   (thinking of a place)
          . . . Philadelphia.

John Ruth from the bar, by Domergue, says loudly;

                    JOHN RUTH
          As long as the bar's Philadelphia, I
          agree.

                                                  CUT TO

EXT—MINNIE'S HABERDASHERY—DAY

We see Maj.Warren and O.B. in this lousy weather remove the
three dead bodies from on top of the stagecoach.

It ain't easy.

The SHOT of Maj.Warren and O.B. starts ZOOMING BACK until we
realize we're looking at them through a window. We continue
to ZOOM BACK FARTHER till we see Oswaldo at the window
watching the men.

CU OSWALDO MOBRAY
The little English man sips his coffy as he watches the two
Americans deal with the dead bodies.

JOE GAGE
lies dozing on a cot.

CHRIS & GENERAL SMITHERS
sit in the two cozy chairs by the fire.

JOHN RUTH (w/Domergue)
Pours himself a cup of coffy from a freshly made pot.

As he drinks he drifts over to the kitchen area, and sees
the discarded HALF PLUCKED CHICKEN.

BOB
Checks the stew, replaces the lid on the top of the pot, and
turns around to face John Ruth (w/Domergue) holding the half
plucked chicken in his hand.

                    JOHN RUTH
                    (meaning the
                    chicken)
          What the hell is this?

                    BOB
          It's a chicken.

                    JOHN RUTH
     No it's not. It's a half plucked chicken.
     A half plucked chicken is bad luck. We
     don't need bad luck in a blizzard. Now
     what's it doing here?

                    BOB
     I was plucking it when your stage arrived.

                    JOHN RUTH
     And you stopped to take care of the
     passengers?

                    BOB
     Si.

                    JOHN RUTH
     Well . . . you're not taking care of the
     passengers now?

                    BOB
     I thought better to deal with the stew.

John Ruth roughly shoves the chicken into Bob's hands;

                    JOHN RUTH
     Pluck the chicken.

Bob takes the chicken and sits down on a stool and finishes
the job of plucking it.

At this point in the story almost everybody has been bullied
by John Ruth at some point or another.

MAJ.WARREN KICKS THE FRONT DOOR OPEN—The WIND from outside
WHIPS INTO THE ROOM—Maj.Warren and O.B. hurry inside and SLAM
the door behind them—Maj.Warren holds the door closed as O.B.
pounds nails into two pieces of wood—nailing the door shut.

When O.B. finishes, he drops the hammer to the floor;

                    O.B.
     That damn door's a dirty whore.

The two freezing men head straight for the pot belly stove
and the coffy pot.

They're so cold they don't even remove their winter coats.

John Ruth picks up the coffy pot and starts pouring the
stagecoach driver and the black man cups.

                    JOHN RUTH
          I just made some more coffy. Git some
          in ya.

They drink the coffy.

                    JOHN RUTH
                    (quietly to
                    Maj.Warren)
          We still got that same deal we talked
          about in the wagon? I help you protect
          your eight thousand, you help me
          protect my ten?

                    MAJ.WARREN
          Yeah, I guess.

                    JOHN RUTH
          One of them fella's
                    (meaning Bob or Joe
                    or Oswaldo or Chris)
          is not what he says he is.

                    O.B.
          What is he?

                    JOHN RUTH
          He's in cahoots with this one
                    (meaning Domergue)
          that's what he is. One of them, maybe
          even two of 'em, is here to see Domergue
          goes free. And to accomplish that goal,
          they'll kill everybody in here.

Maj.Warren looks over to Domergue who hasn't any expression.

                    JOHN RUTH
                    (CON'T)
          And they got 'em a coupla' days. So all
          they gotta' do is sit tight and wait for
          a winda' of opportunity. And that's when
          they strike, huh bitch?

                    DOMERGUE
          If you say so, John.

                    MAJ.WARREN
                    (to John Ruth)
          Are you sure you're not just being
          paranoid?

John Ruth doesn't even entertain the question, he just
continues;

                    JOHN RUTH
          Our best bet is this duplicitous fella'
          ain't as cool a customer as Daisy here.
          He won't have the leather patience it
          takes to just sit here and wait.

                    O.B.
          Wait for what?

                    JOHN RUTH
          An opportunity to kill us all! But
          waiting for an oportunity, and knowing
          it's the right one, isn't so easy. If
          he can't handle it, he'll stop waiting.
          He'll try an' create his opportunity.
          And that's when Mr.Jumpy reveals
          himself. And I bet he does it 'fore
          mornin'. I bet he does it way 'fore
          mornin'.

Maj.Warren turns his head in the direction of Domergue.

                    MAJ.WARREN
          What do you got to say about all this?

                    DOMERGUE
          What do I got to say? About John Ruth's
          ravings? He's absolutely right. Me and
          one of them fella's is in cahoots. And
          we're just waitin' for everybody to go to
          sleep, that's when we gonna' kill y'all.
          Then we just sit tight, drink Mezcal and
          eat stew till the sun comes out.

JOE GAGE
lying down on the cot, with his cowboy hat over his face,
hears the bounty hunter John Ruth call out to the room;

                    JOHN RUTH
          Okay everybody, hear this.

Joe takes the hat away from his face, and remaining
vertical, listens to the bounty hunter's speech.

JOHN RUTH (w/Domergue) stands in the middle of the room,
talking to the other people inside of Minnie's.

JOHN RUTH
(pointing at Domergue)
This here is Daisy Domergue. She's wanted
dead or alive for murder. Ten thousand
dollars. That money's mine boys. Don't
wanna' share it, ain't gonna' lose it.
When the sun comes out, I'm taking this
woman into Red Rock to hang. Now is there
anybody here committed to stopping me
from doing that?

Nobody says anything.

Not Oswaldo Mobray.

Not Joe Gage.

Not Bob.

Not Chris and the Old General.

Not O.B.

Not The Major.

JOHN RUTH
Really? Nobody gotta' problem with this?

Nobody says anything.

John Ruth (taking Domergue with him) slowly crosses the
room;

JOHN RUTH
Well I guess that's very fortunate
for me. However, I hope you will all
understand, I just can't take your
word. Circumstances force me to take
precautions.

When John Ruth stops walking, he's standing at the foot
of Joe Gage's cot, looking down at the reclining
cowboy.

Looking up at the bounty hunter, the cow puncher says;

JOE GAGE
When you say precautions, why do I feel
you mean me?

JOHN RUTH
Because I'm gonna' take your gun, son.

                    JOE GAGE
          You are?

                    JOHN RUTH
          Yes I am. Nothing personal.

                    JOE GAGE
          Just mine? The Hangman got himself a gun?

                    JOHN RUTH
          I'll be dealing with his gun after I
          deal with yours.

Joe Gage raises from his reclined position to a sitting
position, with his hand slowly drifting to the butt of the
pistol on his hip.

                    JOE GAGE
          Feel kinda' naked without it.

John Ruth puts his hand on the butt of his gun, and says;

                    JOHN RUTH
          I still got mine. I'll protect you.

Joe Gage almost can't believe the degree of bastard that is
John Ruth. Still in his sitting position, he places his hand
on the butt of his gun.

Domergue, standing there next to John Ruth, thinks, oh shit.

Joe Gage looking up at John Ruth says;

                    JOE GAGE
          A bastard's work is never done, huh John
          Ruth?

John Ruth looking down at Joe Gage says;

                    JOHN RUTH
          That's right, Joe Gage. Gimmie the gun.

Joe Gage laughs a little to himself at John Ruth's brazen
masculinity, then opens his mouth to say something
cool . . . .

WHEN . . .

Major Warren SWIFTLY COMES UP BEHIND HIM—THROWING HIS ARM
ACROSS HIS NECK—AND A KNIFE BLADE DUG DEEP (but not too
deep) INTO THE SIDE OF JOE GAGE'S NECK.

Joe Gage starts to struggle.

                    MAJ.WARREN
          Calm down.

Joe Gage freezes.

> MAJ.WARREN
> (CON'T)
> Take your hands away from your pistol.

He does.

> MAJ.WARREN
> (CON'T)
> Blink your eyes if you're calm.

Joe Gage BLINKS.

Maj.Warren looks up at John Ruth;

> MAJ.WARREN
> (CON'T)
> Did he blink?

> JOHN RUTH
> He blinked.

> MAJ.WARREN
> (to Joe Gage)
> Blink if you're gonna' remain calm?

Joe Gage BLINKS.

> JOHN RUTH
> He blinked.

> MAJ.WARREN
> Take his gun.

John Ruth reaches down and removes Joe Gage's pistol from the holster on his hip. As he does he tries to soften the blow.

> JOHN RUTH
> I'm real sorry about this, son. Like
> I said, nothing personal. Just a
> precaution.

Maj.Warren takes the knife away, lets go of Joe Gage's neck, and quickly backs away.

Joe doesn't overreact once he's freed.

He touches his throat. Touches the blood running down the side of his neck.

He removes a BANDANA from his pocket, and ties it around his neck where the knife wound was. As he does he glances over his shoulder at Maj.Warren.

                         JOE GAGE
                      (to Maj.Warren)
               Pretty sneaky.

MAJ.WARREN
folds up his knife as he looks back at Joe.

John Ruth approaches Oswaldo the hangman.

                         JOHN RUTH
               I'm afraid the same applies to you too
               Mr.Mobray.

Oswaldo holds open his suit jacket, exposing his pistol in
its holster on his belt, for John Ruth to extract.

                         OSWALDO
               Precautions must be taken because life
               is too sweet to lose.

John Ruth removes the gun from the holster on Mobray's hip.

Then the bounty hunter places both pistols on a table.

John Ruth asks Domergue;

                         JOHN RUTH
               Hand me that little bucket.

She hands him a little bucket.

He takes the two men's pistols apart piece by piece, and
places the pieces in the little bucket. John crumbles the
weapons in his hands like dirt clods.

                         JOHN RUTH
               O.B.?

O.B. steps up.

                         JOHN RUTH
                      (CON'T)
               Go to the outhouse. Dump this bucket
               down the shit hole.

                         O.B.
               Why do I gotta' go outside?

                         JOHN RUTH
               Your jacket's already on. And I sorta
               kinda trust you.

Ruth looks at Joe Gage and Oswaldo Mobray.

                    JOHN RUTH
                     (CON'T)
          When we get to Red Rock I'll replace the
          weapons you lost. That's the best I can
          do. When he leaves, you two nail the
          door behind him.

O.B. takes the little bucket, and YANKS THE FRONT DOOR OPEN—
The WIND from outside WHIPS THROUGH THE ROOM—Oswaldo holds
the door closed as Joe hammers nails into the door.

John Ruth turns to Bob.

                    JOHN RUTH
                     (to Bob)
          Okay Mr.Mex, where's your guns?

                    BOB
          I don't have a gun.

                    JOHN RUTH
          What's that?

John Ruth points at a double barrel shotgun mounted on the
wall.

                    BOB
          Oh well, there's that.

Bob takes the shotgun off the wall and hands it to John
Ruth.

He cracks open the weapon and removes two shotgun shells.
Placing them on a nearby table.

John, holding the shotgun by the barrel, walks to the stone
fireplace, and SMASHES the wooden stock against the stones.
He tosses the useless gun to the floor, and looks to his
audience.

                    JOHN RUTH
          So any more guns I don't know about?
          Now later I'm gonna' remember asking
          this question, and I'm going to
          remember your answer. So, one more
          time, any guns I don't know about?

                    JOE GAGE
          You got 'em all chief. We're your
          prisoners.

                    JOHN RUTH
          Oh don't be so melodramatic, Joe Gage.

Bob steps up.

                    BOB
          I just want to make an announcement.

                    JOHN RUTH
          What announcement?

                    BOB
          Stew's on.

                    JOHN RUTH
          Well then, let's eat.

Everybody except Gen.Smithers moves to the kitchen area.
Chris tries to get the General to come over, but the old
man refuses, preferring to sit in his chair by the fire by
himself.

Bob has laid out a number of bowls, and big brown wooden
spoons.

One by one they go to the stew pot, take the ladle, pour
some stew in the bowl, sit down at the picnic table, and eat.

John Ruth & Domergue.

Chris Mannix.

Major Marquis Warren.

Oswaldo Mobray.

Joe Gage.

and last up, Bob.

INT/EXT—OUTHOUSE—SNOWY DAY

O.B. tosses the pistol pieces down the shit hole.

Then opens the door.

We see how snowy and brutal the weather has become.

He uses the line he and Chris stretched out earlier to make
his way back to Minnie's.

INT—MINNIE'S HABERDASHERY—DAY

Everybody eats in silence. Silence that is except for all
the GOBBLING SOUNDS as they gobble up the stew.

JOHN RUTH & DOMERGUE
are having a little trouble eating with their hands cuffed to
each other. John Ruth takes the TINY HANDCUFF KEY out of his
pocket, and holds it up for his female prisoner to see.

                    JOHN RUTH
          I'm gonna' let you loose while we eat.
          Don't get any ideas, I ain't goin' soft
          on ya'. You lift your ass even one inch
          off this seat, I'll put a bullet right
          in your goddamn throat.

He UNLOCKS the handcuffs.

For the second time in the movie, Domergue's free from Big
John's iron.

THEN . . . .

O.B. KICKS OPEN THE FRONT DOOR, then moves quickly inside
and SLAMS IT SHUT.

Chris jumps up from the table, and helps him hold the door
while O.B. pounds the nails that keep it shut.

As he pounds in the nails O.B. says;

                    O.B.
          Goddamn this fucking fucking whore!

The door's done.

O.B. gets some stew.

Chris sits back down at the table, next to Maj.Warren and
across from John Ruth and Domergue, and starts digging into
his stew bowl.

                    CHRIS
                (as he eats)
          So Domergue, I suppose this blizzard
          counts as a stroke of luck as far as
          you're concerned?

                    DOMERGUE
          You don't hear me complaining
          do ya'?

                    CHRIS
          No I sure don't.
                (to Oswaldo)
          How 'bout you Oswaldo?

                    OSWALDO
          How about me what?

                    CHRIS
          Look, considerin' all the things I done
          for money, I ain't one to judge. But
          don't you feel just the least little bit
          bad 'bout hangin' a woman?

                    OSWALDO
          Till they invent a TRIGGER that women
          can't pull, if you're a hang <u>man</u>, you're
          going to hang <u>women</u>.

                    CHRIS
          Well hell Ozzy, I guess I ain't never
          looked at it like that before.

                    JOHN RUTH
          When it comes to some of them mean
          bastards out there, it's the only thing
          does the job. You really only need to
          hang mean bastards. But mean bastards,
          you need to hang.

                    OSWALDO
          But as I was telling Mr.Ruth and Miss.
          Domergue earlier, I don't like the term
          <u>HANG-MAN</u>. I'm an Executioner. Assuming
          Miss.Domergue has a pain in the neck in
          her future, it won't be me that hangs
          her. It will be the judge, the jury, and
          by extension, the entire town of Red
          Rock that sentences her to hang.
                    (beat)
          <u>I</u> just execute the sentence.

                    CHRIS
          Well I know how ya' feel Ozzy, I don't like
          a lot of the terms John Ruth throws at me.
          But short of shootin' 'em, I don't know a
          hellva' lot I can do about it.

                    JOHN RUTH
          You try shootin' me Mannix, for your
          sake it better be in the back.

                    CHRIS
          Oh don't worry John, it will be.
                    (to Maj.Warren)
          How you doin', black Major?

Major Warren moves his eyes in Chris Mannix's direction,
then moves them back down to his stew bowl.

                    MAJ.WARREN
          I ain't in the mood, Mannix. Leave me
          be from your horseshit.

                    CHRIS
John Ruth says you gotta' Lincoln letter?

Maj.Warren puts down his spoon and turns in his seat to face
Chris.

                    MAJ.WARREN
I tole' you jackass to hee-haw somewhere
else and I meant it.

Chris turns to John Ruth across the table.

                    CHRIS
                    (to John Ruth)
That's right John, you said that didn't ya'?

                    JOHN RUTH
Yes I did.

                    CHRIS
                    (to Maj.Warren)
So....you gotta' letter from Abraham
Lincoln?

                    MAJ.WARREN
Yes.

                    CHRIS
Thee Abraham Lincoln?

                    MAJ.WARREN
Yes.

                    CHRIS
Abraham Lincoln? The President of the
United States...?

                    MAJ.WARREN
Yes.

                    CHRIS
...of America?

                    MAJ.WARREN
Yes.

                    CHRIS
Wrote you a letter, personally?

                    MAJ.WARREN
Yes.

                    CHRIS
Personally? As in; "Dear Maj.Warren"?

                    MAJ.WARREN
No. Personally as in; "Dear Marquis".

                        CHRIS
            "Dear Marquis"?
            Abraham Lincoln-the-President-of-the-
            United-States-of-America?
                        (said as one
                        word)

                        MAJ.WARREN
            Yes.

                        CHRIS
            May I see it?

                        MAJ.WARREN
            No you may not.

                        CHRIS
            But the way John tells it, you weren't
            just some random nigger soldier picked
            from a pile of letters.
                        (beat)
            Way John tells it, y'all hada'
            correspondence.

                        MAJ.WARREN
            Yes.

                        CHRIS
            Way John tells it, y'all's practically
            pen pals?

                        MAJ.WARREN
            Yes.

                        CHRIS
            And a pen pal's.....practically a friend.

Maj.Warren doesn't say anything. He just turns away from
Chris and eats his stew.

Chris turns around to face John Ruth sitting across from him.

                        CHRIS
                        (to John Ruth)
            So you think a nigger drummed outta'
            the Calvary with a yellow stripe down
            his back....was practically friends
            with The President of The United States
            of America?

Now that John Ruth has watched that episode played out in front of him. And frankly, now that he thinks about it, the letter's authenticity does seem unlikely.

> CHRIS
> John Ruth, I hate to be the one to break it to ya', but nobody in Minnie's Haberdashery has ever corresponded with Abraham Lincoln...
> ...Least of all, THAT NIGGER THERE!

John Ruth looks across at Maj.Warren.

Maj.Warren looks back at him.

> JOHN RUTH
> Was that all horseshit?

> MAJ.WARREN
> Course it was.

BEAT.

Then....
> DOMERGUE BURSTS OUT LAUGHING!

John Ruth looks over at her, picks up his stew bowl and THROWS THE STEW IN HER FACE!

Then he turns and faces Maj.Warren sitting across from him.

> JOHN RUTH
> So I guess it's true what they say about you people. You can't believe a fuckin' word that comes outta' your mouths.

> MAJ.WARREN
> What's wrong? I hurt your feelings?

> JOHN RUTH
> As-a-matter-of-fact, you did.

> MAJ.WARREN
> Now I know I'm the only black son-of-a-bitch you ever met, so I'm gonna' cut your ass some slack. But you ain't got no idea what a black man starin' down America looks like.
> (small beat)
> The only time black folks are safe, is when white folks are disarmed.

Pulling the phony letter out of his inside jacket pocket.

> MAJ.WARREN
> This letter had the desired effect of
> disarming white folks.

> JOHN RUTH
> Call it what you want, I call it a dirty
> trick.

He puts the letter back inside his coat.

> MAJ.WARREN
> Wanna' know why I'd lie about something
> like that, white man?
> (beat)
> Got me on that stagecoach, didn't it.

"Yes it did", thinks John Ruth, and the thought makes him
blink.

Maj.Warren suddenly stands up from the table, taking his
stew bowl and spoon with him. As Warren walks away, Chris
says to the table;

> CHRIS
> Well I'll tell you like the lord tole'
> John, a letter from Abraham Lincoln
> wouldn't have that kinda' effect on me.
> I might let a whore piss on it.

General Sanford Smithers sits alone in his grey uniform,
bathed in crackling and cackling FIRE LIGHT.

Maj.Warren walks over to the stew pot, pours some food into
an empty bowl. Picks up a big wooden spoon. Walks over to
where Gen.Smithers sits. And places the stew bowl and spoon
next to him on a little table. Gen.Smithers looks to the
stew bowl, then up at the black fella' in Cavalry pants that
stands over him.

Across the room Chris Mannix yells at Maj.Warren;

> CHRIS
> Warren goddamit, you leave that old man
> alone!

Maj.Warren yells across the room right back;

> MAJ.WARREN
> Stand down you son-of-a-bitch, I shared
> a battlefield with this man.

That makes Chris stand down.

Maj.Warren looks down at the old man in the cozy chair.

> MAJ.WARREN
> Or would you deny me that too?

> GEN.SMITHERS
> I suppose you were there.

Maj.Warren points at the empty cozy chair across from The Old General.

> MAJ.WARREN
> May I join you?

After a clock tick or two, without looking up at him, the old man says;

> GEN.SMITHERS
> Yes you may.

Holding his stew bowl and big wooden spoon, Maj.Warren sits in the chair opposite Gen.Smithers. Maj.Warren is coming correct to the old Southern General, at least as far as the old Southern General is concerned. Correct due to age, due to rank, and due to race.

The two men sit in silence, as Maj.Warren eats a spoonful of stew.

> GEN.SMITHERS
> What's in the stew?

> MAJ.WARREN
> I don't know.
> (yelling to
> Bob)
> Hey Bob! What's in the stew?

Bob answers.

> BOB
> Beaver, buck, and horse.

The Old Man snorts.

> GEN.SMITHERS
> There ain't no buck in that bowl.

The Old Man picks up the spoon and the bowl next to him, and shoves some in his mouth. Then, with some brown stew staining his grey beard, Smithers says;

>   GEN.SMITHERS
>   A lotta' horse. Lotta' possum be my
>   guess.

The two men sit in their chairs by the fire, eating out of their bowls.

Bob finishes at the picnic table, and moseys over to the piano and starts to hesitantly play the Christmas tune "Silent Night".

The two former Civil War officers continue to eat stew with big wooden spoons.

>   MAJ.WARREN
>   How's life been since the war?

>   GEN.SMITHERS
>   Got both of my legs. Got both of my
>   arms. Can't complain.

>   MAJ.WARREN
>   Got a woman?

>   GEN.SMITHERS
>   Fever took her beginning this winter.

>   MAJ.WARREN
>   Me, I never went in for a woman
>   regular.

>   GEN.SMITHERS
>   In my day no one asked you if you went
>   in for it. You just did it.

>   MAJ.WARREN
>   What was her name?

>   GEN.SMITHERS
>   Betsy.

>   MAJ.WARREN
>   Georgia girl?

> GEN.SMITHERS
> Augusta. Atlanta boy, Augusta girl.
> I used to raise Kentucky horses. Her
> paw' owned the breedership I purchased
> most of my ponies from. I made a good
> deal on her. Used that stake I got from
> him. Purchased a few peach orchards.
> Set myself up pretty good. Did a
> hellva' lot better than my no good
> brothers, that's for damn sure. All in
> all....can't complain. Betsy took fat
> after our boy. But I never minded that.
> She was a nice woman, I never minded
> anything she did.

> MAJ.WARREN
> Yeah, your son came up here a coupla'
> years ago. He spoke highly of his mama
> too.

A SHARP STING goes through Sandy Smithers' body as he shifts his focus on the black man.

Just as Bob fucks up "Silent Night", and starts again.

> GEN.SMITHERS
> You knew my boy?

> MAJ.WARREN
> Did I know 'em?
> (small chuckle)
> Yeah....I knew 'em.

The old man snorts.

> GEN.SMITHERS
> You didn't know 'em.

Maj.Warren places his stew bowl aside, and says;

> MAJ.WARREN
> Fine, suit yourself.

Maj.Warren stands and the old man grabs his wrist.

> GEN.SMITHERS
> Didja' know my boy?

Maj.Warren looks down at the frantic old man, and says calmly;

> MAJ.WARREN
> I know the day he died, do you?

The old man is hit in the heart. He croaks out a;

                    GEN.SMITHERS
          No.

Looking down at the feeble old man in the chair;

                    MAJ.WARREN
          Wanna' know what day that was?

The old man clutches the black man's sleeve tighter.

                    GEN.SMITHERS
          Yes.

The black man leans down slightly closer to the old man, and says;

                    MAJ.WARREN
          The day he met me.

The white old man falls back in his chair.

As Bob continues to play "Silent Night" more confidently,
the black bounty hunter removes one of his pistols from his
gun belt, and places it on the little table next to Sandy
Smithers' chair.

The old man looks down at it.

Then, with one pistol left in his gun belt, Maj.Warren walks
over to the bar in Philadelphia, leans against it sideways,
and continues talking to the old man in Georgia.

                    MAJ.WARREN
          He came up here to do a little nigger
          head huntin'. By then the reward was
          five thousand and bragging rights. But
          back then to battle hard rebs, five
          thousand just to cut off a nigger's
          head, that was good money. So the
          Johnny's climbed this mountain, lookin'
          for fortune. But there was no fortune
          to be found. All they found was me.
          All them fella's came up here, when
          they found themselves at the mercy of
          a nigger's gun, sang a different tune.
          "Let's just forget it. I go my way,
          you go yours", that's your boy Chester
          talkin'.

The old man by the fire SCREAMS AT HIM from across the room;

                    GEN.SMITHERS
          You a damn lie!

                MAJ.WARREN
"If you just let me go home to my
family, I'll never set foot in Wyoming
again", that's what they all said. Some
of them ole' boys had some real sad
stories to tell too.
            (beat)
Beggin' for his life, your boy told me
his WHOLE LIFE STORY. And you was in
that story, General. And when I knew
me I had the boy of The Bloody Nigger
Killer of Baton Rouge....I knew me I
was gonna' have some fun.

The other people, most of which are still around the picnic
table, know exactly what Maj.Warren is doing. He's placed a
loaded pistol by the old man, and now is trying to provoke
Gen.Smithers to pick it up, and point it at the black man. At
which point the black man can legally shoot him dead in self
defense.

Chris Mannix is on his feet YELLING at the black man and the
old white man;

                CHRIS
           (to Maj.Warren)
You shut your lyin' nigger lips up!
           (to Gen.Smithers)
Gen.Smithers, don't listen to 'em, he
don't know your boy! He just heard tell
why you here is all! He's just peckin'
at ya' for a fight!

                MAJ.WARREN
           (to Gen.Smithers)
It was cold the day I killed your boy.
And I don't mean snowy mountain in
Wyoming cold...Colder than that. And
on that cold day, with your boy at the
business end of my gun barrel....
...I made him STRIP. Right down to
his <u>bare</u> <u>ass</u>. Then I told him to start
walkin'.

FLASH TO

EXT—SNOWY VISTA IN THE MOUNTAINS—DAY

We see what Maj.Warren describes. But we see the BIG WIDE
70MM SUPER CINEMASCOPE VERSION.

A magnificient white Wyoming winter vista, and inside of it, Maj.Warren on his horse Lash, pointing a rifle at A NAKED WHITE MAN walking ahead of him in the snow.

                    MAJ.WARREN VOICE (OS)
          I walked his naked ass for two hours....

Then we see the naked White Man collapse in the snow.

Maj.Warren holds up his horse, and watches the cold man.

                    MAJ.WARREN VOICE (OS)
          ....'fore the cold collapsed him.

BACK TO MINNIE'S

CU GEN.SMITHERS

                    GEN.SMITHERS
          You never knew my boy!

Chris joins in;

                    CHRIS
          No he didn't! He's just a sneaky nigger
          tryin' to getcha to go for that gun!
          This black devil's a bounty hunter,
          that's how bounty hunters do!

Maj.Warren just continues with his story. His concentration unaffected by the other voices in the room.

                    MAJ.WARREN
          Then he started in begging again. But
          this time he wasn't begging to go home.
          He knew he'd never see his home again.
          And he wasn't beggin' for his life no
          more. That was long gone and he knew
          it. He was just beggin' for a BLANKET.
          Now don't judge your son too harshly.
          You ain't never been as cold as your boy
          was that day. You'd be surprised what a
          man that cold, would-do-for-a-blanket.
          Wanna' know what your boy did?

The old man watches the storyteller, eyes bulging out of his head.

                    MAJ.WARREN
                    (pause)
          I took my big black pecker outta' my
          pants. And I made him crawl in the snow
          on all fours over to it. Then I grabbed
          a hand full of that black hair on the
          back of his head.....

The old man leans forward in his chair.

                    MAJ.WARREN
          Then I stuck that big black johnson
          right down his goddamn throat. And
          that johnson was fulla' blood. So
          it was warm. You bet your sweet ass it
          was warm. And Chester Charles Smithers
          sucked on that warm black dingus as
          long as he could.

FLASH ON

EXT—SNOWY VISTA—DAY

We see what Maj.Warren describes in BIG WIDE 70MM SUPER
CINEMASCOPE.

A WHITE WINTER WYOMING VISTA, and inside of that vista, is a
Naked White Man on his knees sucking the dick of a Heavily
Clothed Black Man in the snow.

BACK TO MINNIE'S

CU GEN.SMITHERS
the old man is in knots. It was worse than his imagination
ever dared.

He knows the truth when he hears it. This is how Chester
ended his life.

CU MAJ.WARREN
the black Major has the white General right where he wants
him. He flashes an alligator grin, and says;

                    MAJ.WARREN
          Starting to see pictures, ain't ya'?
          Your son. Black dude's dingus in his
          mouth. Him shiverin'—him cryin'—me
          laughin'—him not understandin'. But you
          understand, doncha' Sandy?
                    (beat)
          I never did give your boy that blanket.
          Even after all he did, and he did
          everything I asked. No blanket. That
          blanket was just a heart breakin' liar's
          promise. Sorta' like when the union issued
          those colored troopers uniforms....that
          you chose not to acknowledge.

Maj.Warren makes his point.

It's a pretty good one.

MAJ.WARREN
So what are you gonna' do old man? You
gonna' spend the next two or three
days ignoring the nigger who killed
your boy? Ignoring how I made him
suffer? Ignoring the agony I inflicted?
Ignoring how I made him lick all over
my johnson? Yep', the dumbest thing
your boy ever did, was let me know he
was your boy.

The Old Man LEAPS TO HIS FEET GRABBING THE GUN, bringing the
pistol's barrel up towards Maj.Warren at the bar.

Barely even turning towards him, Maj.Warren calmly and
smoothly pulls his pistol from his holster, and puts a bullet
square in the Old Man's chest.

Maj.Warren's pistol BLOWS GEN.SMITHERS OFF HIS FEET and INTO
THE ROARING FIREPLACE.

His old uniform CATCHES FIRE, and he FLIP FLOPS on the floor,
letting out a HIGH PITCHED SCREAM as The Old Man burns.

Some of the people at Minnie's run to put out the fire.

Maj.Warren DRAWS HIS GUN stopping them.

MAJ.WARREN
Let 'em burn.

And burn he does.

Till he's dead.

CHRIS
We gotta' put it out 'fore it burns this
whole place down!

Major Marquis replaces his pistol back in its holster.

MAJ.WARREN
Go ahead.

They put out the blazing body till it's just a smoldering
corpse.

CUT TO BLACK

Chapter Four

Domergue's got a secret

CUT FROM BLACK TO:
OVERHEAD CRANE SHOT OF MINNIE'S HABERDASHERY

We see an overhead tableaux of Minnie's Haberdashery about
fifteen minutes since the last page.

Maj.Warren sits at a table alone, drinking from the Brandy
bottle.

Both Joe Gage and O.B. carry the dead burnt corpse of
Gen.Smithers out of the room and out the door. The WIND
from outside WHIPS INTO THE ROOM—Bob shuts the door behind
them—CUTTING OFF THE WIND—and holds it closed.

Domergue (still unchained) hasn't moved from her spot
before. She still sits at the community picnic table.

An unseen LITERARY NARRATOR comes on the soundtrack clueing
the audience in to what's happening.

                    NARRATOR (VO)
          About fifteen minutes has passed since
          we last left our characters. During
          that time Chris, John Ruth, and Oswaldo
          got into a vigorous debate about the
          legality of what just transpired. Marquis
          Warren, who is supremely confident about
          the legality of what just transpired,
          ignored them, sat at a table by himself
          and finished the brandy bottle. Then as
          the legality discussion started to wind
          down due to lack of oxygen, Joe Gage and
          O.B. carried the dead charred body of
          Gen.Smithers out of the haberdashery to
          stash out in the snow. Bob held the door
          for them. Domergue, however, hasn't moved
          from her spot at the community dinner
          table since John Ruth uncuffed her.

The CAMERA begins to CRANE DOWN towards Domergue till it
LANDS on a TIGHT MEDIUM of her.

                    NARRATOR (VO)
          At this point in the story Daisy Domergue
          is keen with anticipation. Something
          her face, body, and demeanor are trying
          very hard to conceal. Because, as stated
          in the title of this Chapter Four,
          Domergue's got a secret.

FREEZE FRAME on Domergue.

                    NARRATOR (VO)
          Let's go back a bit.

                                                    CUT TO

INT—MINNIE'S HABERDASHERY—DAY

We've gone back in time to the moment Maj.Warren was
taunting the Old Man by telling him tales of sticking his
dick down the General's son's throat. Except this time we
watch the scene from an eye level perspective across the
room...more or less in the area of the pot belly stove.

                    NARRATOR (VO)
               Fifteen minutes ago Maj.Warren shot
               Gen.Smithers in front of everybody.
               But....twenty seconds before that,
               something equally as important
               happened, but not everybody saw it.

The CAMERA BEGINS MOVING BACK......Till......The pot
belly stove and The BLUE COFFY POT enter FRAME.

Maj.Warren talking shit across the room a little SOFT in the
B.G. and The Blue Coffy Pot on the RIGHT SIDE OF FRAME SHARP
in the F.G.

                    NARRATOR (VO)
               You see, while Warren was reminiscing
               with Smithers about his boy...

WE SEE UNSEEN FINGERS lift the LID off of the blue coffy
pot.

                    NARRATOR (VO)
               ...somebody...

WE SEE UNSEEN FINGERS pour the contents of a LITTLE BLUE
BLACK BOTTLE into the coffy pot.

                    NARRATOR (VO)
               ...poisoned the coffy.

                                                  CUT TO

CU DOMERGUE
And the only one to see him do it was Domergue. Her head is
turned away from the black Major, her eyes are big saucers, as
she watches The Poisoner poison the coffy.

                    NARRATOR (VO)
               And the only one was to see 'em do it,
               was Domergue.

OFF SCREEN The Poisoner locks eyes with Domergue.

Domergue looks back . . .

When . . .

BANG!

Domergue turns around at the shot fired behind her, we see from her perspective Gen.Smithers blown into the fireplace.

PICNIC TABLE
We see the people around the table (except for Domergue) rise and start to move towards the fire.

WE SEE MAJ.WARREN'S PISTOL COME FROM OFF FRAME—POINT AND COCK AT THE PEOPLE INSIDE.

The People freeze.

> MAJ.WARREN (OS)
> Let 'em burn.

The people can't take their eyes off of the burning Smithers . . . .
. . . all except Domergue . . . who sneaks a look behind her.

DOMERGUE'S POV:
Her perspective of the deadly blue coffy pot of poison . . . just sitting on the stove . . . waiting to be deadly.

                                                    CUT TO

BACK TO THE PRESENT

DOMERGUE
The CAMERA MOVES INTO A CU OF DOMERGUE with just the barest hint of a smile on her face.

                                                    CUT TO

EXT—MINNIE'S HABERDASHERY—SUNSET

Joe Gage and O.B. have tossed the corpse of Gen.Smithers out in the woods. As they go back to the shelter they realize the sky is magnificently beautiful, windy, but beautiful. The SUNSET paints ice cream colors not only in the sky but against the surrounding white snow. With both the wind and the cold whipping around them, Joe Gage and O.B. take in the sight.

Enjoying it.

                                                    CUT TO

INT—MINNIE'S HABERDASHERY—SUNSET

The BLUE COFFY POT
ON THE RIGHT SIDE OF FRAME sits the Blue Deadly Coffy pot on
the stove. ON THE LEFT SIDE OF FRAME the camera is pointed at
the front door in the B.G.

The front door opens, and Joe Gage and O.B. walk through it.

Bob slams the door, and goes about nailing it shut.

The very cold O.B. makes a beeline towards the blue coffy
pot.

Joe Gage heads for the fireplace to warm up instead.

John Ruth, by the pot belly stove, lifts the blue coffy pot
off of the stove and pours the stagecoach driver a cup.

Right after it gets poured, O.B. brings it up to his lips and
DRINKS IT.

John Ruth pours himself a cup, then replaces the blue coffy
pot back on the hot stove.

O.B. heads over to the bar, to light candles and lanterns
now it's getting darker.

John Ruth takes the untouched coffy cup, and crosses the
room back over to the picnic dinner table that Domergue is
sitting at.

He takes a DRINK OF POISON COFFY as he sits down next to
Domergue.

Domergue watches him do it, and can't help but smile.

John Ruth sees her smile at him.

He holds out the coffy cup, offering her some;

                    JOHN RUTH
            Want some?

                    DOMERGUE
            No thanks. It's getting late. Coffy
            makes me jumpy.

                    JOHN RUTH
            You look a little jumpy. Must be all
            this Freedom.

He puts down the coffy cup, grabs her arm and LOCKS himself
back in the handcuff attached to her wrist.

                    DOMERGUE
          Awww John, I thought—

                    JOHN RUTH
          —You thought wrong, bitch.

                    DOMERGUE
          If you just give me a chance—

                    JOHN RUTH
          —Bitch, you had your chance.

Then DRINKS MORE COFFY.

Domergue giggles.

She has to play it cool, but each drink he takes is like a
knife plunge.

John Ruth TAKES ANOTHER DRINK.

Domergue smiles a satisfied smile, turns away and her eyes
search for O.B.

She finds O.B. walking around the shack LIGHTING CANDLES and
LANTERNS. Bob and Chris do the same as the LIGHTING turns
from DAY TO NIGHT.

DOMERGUE
watches.

O.B.
lights a lantern. He seems fine. He walks over to where Chris
is lighting six candles in a candle holder. He removes a
candle, and lights more candles with it.

DOMERGUE
watches O.B.

Behind her we see the pot belly stove with the blue coffy
pot on it in SOFT FOCUS in the B.G. We also see Chris enter
this soft focus lighting candles.

O.B.
lights more candles.
We SLOWLY ZOOM TOWARDS HIM.

DOMERGUE
watches O.B. . . . waiting.

Behind her we see Chris in SOFT FOCUS pick up the blue coffy
pot and pour a cup.

O.B.
puts down his candle, and picks up his coffy cup taking a big
drink. We ZOOM CLOSER TOWARDS HIM.

DOMERGUE
watches O.B....waiting....WHEN...

John Ruth, handcuffed to Domergue, GUTS EXPLODE INSIDE OF
HIM VOMITING BLOOD.

In the B.G. Chris with the coffy cup in hand, stops and
looks.

O.B.
turns and looks.

JOHN RUTH
holds his belly. Looks at the puke in front of him, sees it's
blood. He doesn't get it.

THEN....

O.B.'s
GUTS EXPLODE INSIDE OF HIM VOMITING BLOOD. Knocking him to
all fours on the floor.

JOHN RUTH
Guts explode again, VOMITING MORE BLOOD.

O.B.
on all fours VOMITS MORE BLOOD on the floor.

JOHN RUTH
is ready to collapse from the picnic table. He looks over to
the woman he is chained to and sees Domergue's smiling face.

Domergue smiles and bats her eyes at him.

                    DOMERGUE
          When you get to hell, John?
          Tell 'em Daisy sent ya'.

John Ruth realizes Domergue's got a secret.

She's killed him.

ROARING like a dragon, John Ruth rises to his feet, and
takes his big fist and PUNCHES DAISY RIGHT SQUARE IN THE
MOUTH.

Her head SNAPS VIOLENTLY BACK, as her lips EXPLODE BLOOD.
When Domergue's head comes back, she SPITS OUT HER TWO FRONT
TEETH, and laughs at him.

John Ruth quickly turns to Chris Mannix with the cup of
coffy in his hand;

                    JOHN RUTH
          Mannix, the coffy!

Everybody in the room hears this.

Mannix throws his coffy cup to the floor, undrunk.

Ruth turns back to Domergue's laughing bloody face . . . . . and
PUNCHES it again, knocking her to the floor.

Daisy continues to laugh, as he climbs on top of her,
grabbing a handful of her hair with one hand, and bringing
his other fist SMASHING IN HER FACE.

THEN . . . .

The poison hits John Ruth's guts again, he RETCHES . . . . and
PUKES BLOODY ALL OVER DAISY.

Daisy just laughs . . . . .

His guts turn more . . . .

He PUKES MORE BLOOD . . . .

The pain in his guts makes him roll off of her on to the
floor holding his sides . . . he weakly takes out his pistol
from the holster on his hip . . . . she grabs at it . . . . chained
together they struggle over the gun . . .

Everybody watches the struggle on the floor.

His guts retch again . . . he doubles over . . . leaving Domergue
the pistol . . . she holds it with both hands . . . . She cocks
back the hammer . . .

And FIRES THREE SHOTS into John Ruth's chest and body.

The big bad bounty hunter tips over to the floor dead.

One of Maj.Warren's hands grabs Domergue by the hair, the
other grabs the gun and wrestles it away from her grip, then
hits her in the head with it, knocking her back.

THEN . . . .

MAJ.WARREN
turns the pistol on everybody else in the room.

                    MAJ.WARREN
          Everybody get your back sides up
          against that back wall!

                    JOE GAGE
              Look goddamit—

Maj.Warren FIRES his pistol.

The bullet STRIKES the top of a wooden chair, right beside
Joe Gage's hand. The WOOD EXPLODES right next to Joe Gage's
flesh, burning, stinging, cutting, and shocking him.

Gage jumps back, holding his stinging hand, looking at
Maj.Warren.

                    MAJ.WARREN
              Get or don't get Gage. It's up to you.

                    JOE GAGE
              I'll get.

                    MAJ.WARREN
              Then get.

Joe Gage gets up against the wall with the other men in the
room.

Chris Mannix, Oswaldo Mobray, Joe Gage, and Bob stand in a
line, backs to the wall.

Domergue sits on the ground, wrist still handcuffed to the
wrist of the dead bad ass John Ruth.

MAJ.WARREN
two guns in hand, one of his own, the other John Ruth's, a
third in the holster on his hip, keeps them pointed at the
four men.

Maj.Warren looks down at O.B.

Dead.

He looks to John Ruth and Domergue on the floor.

One dead, one stares back with hate.

Then he looks to the four men he has lined up against the wall.

                    MAJ.WARREN
                  (to the room)
              Y'all keep your mouth shut and do what
              I tell ya'. Anybody opens their mouth,
              gonna' get a bullet. Anybody moves a
              little weird....little sudden—gonna'
              get a bullet. Not a warning. Not a
              question. A bullet. Now y'all got that?

They acknowledge.

Using John Ruth's line, the Major says;

>   MAJ.WARREN
> Let me hear you say, "I got it".

He makes them say it.

>   MAJ.WARREN
> Mannix?

Chris Mannix's eyes go to him.

>   MAJ.WARREN
> Get over on this side.

Chris moves cautiously away from the wall, to the Major's side of the room.

>   MAJ.WARREN
> Take that pistol out of this holster.

Indicating the pistol still in the left side holster hanging from the Major's hip.

Chris looks at him with an expression that says; "Really?"

The Major nods affirmative.

Chris cautiously removes the pistol from the black man's belt.

Now Chris has a gun. He looks to the Major, who still has two guns pointed at the other three men against the wall.

>   MAJ.WARREN
> Okay, point it at them. Like I said,
> they do anything—and I mean "anything"—
> kill 'em.

Chris Mannix does that.

>   CHRIS
>   (to Maj.Warren)
> So you finally decided I'm tellin' the
> truth 'bout bein' the sheriff of Red
> Rock, huh?

>   MAJ.WARREN
>   (to Chris)
> I don't know 'bout all that. But you
> ain't the killer who poisoned that
> coffy. You almost drunk it your own
> damn self.

The Major's eyes go back to the three men against the wall.

                    MAJ.WARREN
                    (to them)
          But one of y'all is.

The Major hears something, and he turns towards Domergue on
the floor.

She has dug the TINY HANDCUFF KEY out of John Ruth's pocket,
and is just about to stick it in the lock and free herself
from the corpse...WHEN...

Maj.Warren points one of his pistols at her, and FIRES into
the FLOOR next to her. The SOUND in the enclosed log cabin
is eardrum exploding LOUD. She freezes.

Maj.Warren, his one arm outstretched, holding a gun pointed
at the three men against the wall. The other arm is holding
a gun pointed at Domergue on the floor. He takes the gun
pointed at Domergue, and places it back in its holster. Then
he holds his hand out, palm up to Domergue.

                    MAJ.WARREN
          Gimmie the key.

It breaks her heart, but she places the tiny handcuff key in
the palm of his hand, his fingers close around it.

Maj.Warren walks across the room to the pot belly stove. He
opens the door of the stove above the fire, and TOSSES THE
TINY KEY INSIDE.

Domergue, whose modus operandi is outrageous behavior and
the disarming affect it has on opponents, can't believe
Marquis just did what he did. She SCREAMS AT HIM;

                    DOMERGUE
          YOU MOTHERFUCKING BLACK BASTARD! You're
          gonna' die on this mountain and I'm
          gonna' fucking laugh when you do!

Maj.Warren turns from the stove and FIRES his pistol at
Domergue.

The BULLET EXPLODES in the dead body of John Ruth next to
her, SHOWERING HER WITH RUTH'S BLOOD. It shocks her enough
to shut her up.

                    MAJ.WARREN
          What I say 'bout talkin'? 'Meant it,
          didn't I?
                    (more)

                    MAJ.WARREN
                     (CON'T)
          You need to understand. You just shot
          the only man committed to getting you
          to Red Rock alive. Raise your voice
          again, and the next bullet goes in your
          lung.

Major Warren has all the attention in the room. He turns
from her on the floor, to them against the wall.

                    MAJ.WARREN
          Now...one of you....<u>is</u> workin' with
          her. Or...two of you <u>are</u> workin'
          with her. Or...<u>all y'all</u> is workin'
          with her. But only one of you poisoned
          the coffy.
                     (gesturing towards
                     Domergue)
          Now whatever charms this bitch got
          make you brave a blizzard and kill
          in cold blood, I'm sure I don't know.
          But....John Ruth's trying to hang your
          woman, so you kill him...okay—maybe?
          But O.B. wasn't hangin' nobody. He's
          sure enough dead now though, ain't he?
          Just like any one of us who'd drank that
          coffy.
                     (to the three)
          Those of you against the wall don't
          practice in poison should think about
          that. Think about how that coulda' been
          you rollin' around on the floor. And
          about how one of the men next ta' ya'
          is responsible.

Chris chimes in;

                    CHRIS
          And I know who I got my money on.
                     (to Joe Gage)
          Yeah that's right cow puncher, I'm
          lookin' at you.

                    MAJ.WARREN
                     (to Chris)
          Not so fast Chris. We'll get there.
          Let's slow it down. Let's slow it way
          down.
                     (to the three)
          Who made the coffy?

Bob, pointing at the dead bounty hunter on the floor, says;

                    BOB
          He did.

                    CHRIS
          Yeah, he did didn't he?

                    MAJ.WARREN
          Yes he did.

The Major thinks silently for a moment.

They watch him think.

Then he says;

                    MAJ.WARREN
                    (CON'T)
          Why is "The Hangman", who's got nothing
          on his mind except gettin' this girl
          to the gallows, brewin' the coffy at
          Minnie's Haberdashery?

The Little English Man points at The Mexican Man.

                    OSWALDO
          Because his coffy was dreadful.

                    MAJ.WARREN
                    (to Bob)
          Really? Well ain't that interesting.

                    BOB
                    (to Maj.Warren)
          You didn't have any of my coffy, bounty
          hunter. So don't be so sure about what
          this little man says.

                    JOE GAGE
          I had his coffy. Wasn't the best coffy I
          ever drank, but wasn't nothin' wrong with it.

                    BOB
          If you want me to make a pot of coffy,
          all you have to do is ask?

                    MAJ.WARREN
          Maybe...maybe...but it's the stew got
          me thinking. When did you say Minnie
          left? A week ago?

                    BOB
          Si.

                    MAJ.WARREN
        See, when my mama made stew, it always
        tasted the same, no matter the meat.
        And there was another fellow on the
        plantation, Uncle Charly, and he made
        stew too. And just like my mama's, I ate
        his stew from the time I was a whipper
        to a full grown man. And no matter
        the meat, it always tasted like Uncle
        Charly's stew. Now I ain't had Minnie's
        stew in 'bout six months or so, so I
        ain't no expert. But that damn sure was
        Minnie's stew. So...if Minnie's on the
        north side visiting her mama...how'd
        she make the stew this morning?

Maj.Warren moves over to the cozy chair he sat in opposite
General Smithers earlier. It's covered in a blanket and a few
animal skins.

                    MAJ.WARREN
        This is Sweet Dave's chair. When I sat in
        it earlier, I couldn't believe it. Nobody
        sits in Sweet Dave's chair. I mean this
        may be Minnie's place, but this damn sure
        is Sweet Dave's chair. If Sweet Dave <u>did</u>
        go to the north side, I'm pretty goddamn
        sure that chair's going with him.

He removes the skins and blanket that cover the chair. The
cloth patterned chair has a BIG BLOOD STAIN on it.

Maj.Warren looks to the room for a reaction.

                    BOB
        So are you actually accusing me of murder?

                    MAJ.WARREN
        Well Bob, it's like this. Whoever's
        workin' with her,
                    (meaning Domergue)
        ain't who they say they are. If it's
        you, that means Minnie and her man
        ain't at her mama's. They're lyin' out
        back there dead somewhere.
                    (to Oswaldo)
        Or if it's you British Man, the real
        Oswaldo Mobray is lyin' in a ditch
        somewhere. And you're just an English
        fella' passin' off his papers.

                    CHRIS
                    (to Joe Gage)
        Or we go by my theory, which is the
        ugliest guy did it. Which makes it you,
        Joe Gage.

                    BOB
                (to Maj.Warren)
So I take it you've deduced the coffy
was poisoned while you were murdering
the old man?

                    MAJ.WARREN
Yes.

                    BOB
Well during that whole incident, I
was sitting on that side of the room,
playing Silent Night on the piano.

The piano couldn't be further from the pot belly stove.

                    MAJ.WARREN
                (to Bob)
I didn't say you poisoned the coffy. I
said you didn't make the stew.
                (to all)
My THEORY is . . . . . You're working with
the man who poisoned the coffy. And
both of you murdered Minnie, and Sweet
Dave, and anybody else mighta' picked
the wrong day to visit the Haberdashery
this morning. And your intention was,
at some point, ambush John Ruth and
free Daisy. But you didn't expect the
blizzard, and you didn't expect the two
of us.
                    (using the barrel of
                    his pistol to
                    indicate both him
                    and Chris)
That's as far as I got. How am I doin'?

                    BOB
You're a real imaginative nigger, ain't
you? So do you intend to murder me
based on a far fetched nigger theory?
Or can you prove it, cabrón?

                    MAJ.WARREN
It ain't so far fetched, Bob.
And it's a bit more than theory.
                (beat)
When did you start workin' for Minnie?

                    BOB
Four months ago.

                    MAJ.WARREN
        Well if you worked here two and a half
        years ago, you'da known all about the
        sign usta' hang above the bar.

Bob doesn't know what he's talking about.

                    MAJ.WARREN (CON'T)
        Minnie never mentioned it?

                    BOB
        No.

                    MAJ.WARREN
        You know what that sign said, Bob?

Bob doesn't say anything.

                    MAJ.WARREN (CON'T)
        It said; "NO DOGS OR MEXICANS ALLOWED".
        Minnie hung up that sign the day she
        opened The Haberdashery. And it hung up
        there every day till they took it down
        a little more than two years ago. You
        know why they took it down?
                (beat)
        They started lettin' in dogs.

Bob doesn't say anything.

                    MAJ.WARREN (CON'T)
        Minnie likes everybody. But she sure
        don't like Mexicans. So you tell me
        Minnie went to the North side to
        visit her mama? Well I find that
        highly unlikely...but okay—maybe?
        But you tell me Minnie Mink took The
        Haberdashery, the most precious thing
        to her in the world, and put it in the
        hands of a Goddamn Mexican?
        Well that's what I meant when I said;
        "That sure don't sound like Minnie?"
        Now I am calling you a liar, Senor Bob.
        And if you're lying, which you are, that
        means you killed Minnie...

Maj.Warren SHOOTS BOB in the chest, the bullet goes through
him, EXPLODING BLOOD and GUNK AGAINST THE BACK WALL.

                    MAJ.WARREN (CON'T)
        ...and you killed Sweet Dave...

Maj.Warren SHOOTS BOB AGAIN, BLOWING HIM BACK AGAINST THE WALL.

Bob's body does a bloody slide to the floor.

Maj.Warren points his pistol at the face of the corpse on the floor that was once Bob.

                    MAJ. WARREN (CON'T)
          And more than likely the driver of
          that stagecoach out there.

Maj.Warren SHOOTS his pistol, destroying the face of Bob.

Then the black Major brings up his smoking pistol barrel and points it in the direction of the two men left.

                    MAJ.WARREN (CON'T)
          Three measly bullets...and there goes
          Bob. But that still don't get us any
          closer to which of you two poisoned the
          coffy, does it Chris?

                    CHRIS
          No it sure don't.

Maj.Warren crosses away from them...

                    MAJ.WARREN
          Now one of y'all poisoned the coffy to
          free Daisy.

....and over to the pot belly stove.

He picks up the coffy pot.

                    MAJ.WARREN (CON'T)
          If I don't hear a confession from one of
          you motherfuckers quick, fast, and in
          a hurry...I'm gonna' pour this whole
          pot of coffy down that bitch's goddamn
          throat.

No response from Oswaldo or Joe Gage.

                    MAJ.WARREN (CON'T)
          Okay, time's up.

He takes the coffy pot and crosses heading towards Daisy.

Joe Gage shouts out.

                    JOE GAGE
          Stop!

Warren stops in place.

                    JOE GAGE (CON'T)
          All right. I done it. I poisoned the
          coffy.

Chris Mannix explodes;

                    CHRIS
          I fucking knew it! You gonna' die now
          you murdering bastard!

While Chris Mannix rages at Joe Gage, the CAMERA drops
down from behind Major Warren, from head to foot and even
past that, through the floorboards to the basement below—
revealing JODY with a gun in hand pointed up at Maj.Warren,
standing directly above him.

                    JODY
          Say Adios to your Huevos.

He FIRES—the flash of gunfire momentarily lights up the
basement.

The bullet from Jody's gun rips through Maj.Warren's groin,
exploding his balls. The Major SCREAMS like someone whose
balls have just been shot off.

CHRIS
jerks his head around to see what happened.

                    CHRIS
          Major Warren...

Oswaldo quickly whips out a hidden pistol...

He fires at Chris.

The bullet rips into Chris. But he manages to get off a shot
at Oswaldo as he goes down.

Chris' bullet rips into Oswaldo's chest. He goes down.

Oswaldo writhes on the ground at the wall, his chest burning
with pain, bleeding profusely.

Chris, too, is on the ground, trembling, bleeding—but still
with gun in hand. He points it at Joe Gage.

Joe Gage raises his hands in surrender.

                    JOE GAGE
          I ain't got no gun. All right?

He takes his hat off and turns around, hands in the air.

MAJ.WARREN
Shot in the balls, alive, screaming in pain, unable to get off
the floor.

                                        CUT TO BLACK

Chapter Five

The Four Passengers

CUT FROM BLACK:

MEDIUM SHOT JESUS STATUE
Same statue as before but earlier that morning before the
blizzard. When the sky above it was bright blue and the snow
capped mountains in the B.G. were at their most majestic, and
BEFORE THE SNOW CANOPY overtook it.

A six horse pulled stagecoach comes roaring past.

CUT TO

EXT—MINNIE'S HABERDASHERY—MORNING

It's the same day at Minnie's, except early morning. It's cold
as hell, but the storm hasn't hit yet, so the sun's out and
it's amazing looking in 70MM SUPERSCOPE.

A SUBTITLE READS:

                    "Earlier that morning at Minnie's"

A six horse team led stagecoach comes roaring up to Minnie's
place. The same stagecoach O.B. noticed earlier, pulled off
to the side. Up on the driver's seat perch sits Two Drivers,
ED (a big older shitkicker type) and SIX-HORSE JUDY (a young
female Calamity Jane type, dressed in buckskin). Judy's on
reins, she pulls the horses to a stop in front of Minnie's.

A chubby half Black, half Indian boy wearing a winter coat
comes running out of Minnie's. His name is CHARLY, he works
there.

The two drivers up on their perch look down at young Charly.

                         ED
               Hey Charly my boy, how the hell are you?

                         CHARLY
               Hi ya' Ed, hi ya' Judy. How many ya'
               got?

                         ED
               Full house today, friend.

                         CHARLY
               We got one in there waiting.

                         ED
               Well he's gonna' hafta keep on waitin'
               cause we ain't got no room.

                         CHARLY
               Well you need to tell Minnie. Cause he's
               been here two days, and Minnie wants
               him outta' here.

                         ED
               Well I can't give him a seat I don't have—
                         (interrupts himself,
                         turns to Judy)
               Take the passengers inside, introduce
               them to Minnie. Warm yourself up. Drink
               some coffy.

Judy jumps off her perch onto the ground.

She looks into the stagecoach door window. Judy being from
New Zealand speaks with a Kiwi accent.

                    JUDY
          Here we are everybody, Minnie's
          Haberdashery. Step outside, you and
          your friends can stretch your legs.
          When you're ready, step on inside, get
          warm by the fire, get some coffy in
          you. I'll introduce you to Minnie.

Judy bounces into Minnie's. We haven't seen the four
passengers yet.

INSERT The DOOR HANDLE
of the stagecoach door, turns. The door opens, the CAMERA
PANS down to the Foot Step right below the stagecoach door. A
Boot steps on it. Then Another, and Another, and Another. All
stepping on to foot fall and out of frame.

INT—MINNIE'S HABERDASHERY—MORNING

It's early morning at Minnie's Haberdashery, the business
part of the building just opening for business.

Minnie herself is in the kitchen area. On this mountain the
black woman named MINNIE MINK is a beloved figure. Everybody
on this mountain knows her, and knows her Haberdashery.

Sitting in his chair that Maj.Warren talked about is SWEET
DAVE. He's Minnie's something. No one knows for sure what
they are to each other. Rumor has it Minnie used to be Sweet
Dave's slave. And after Minnie got her freedom, Sweet Dave
didn't want to live without her. And if she'd stay with him,
he'd buy her a place of her own, she could run anyway she
wants. But that's only a rumor.

Sweet Dave sits in one of the two cozy chairs by the fire,
playing CHESS with GENERAL SMITHERS sitting in the chair we
first found him in.

A pretty young black gal with an incredibly sweet smile is
in the kitchen area plucking a chicken, her name is GEMMA.

Judy sits on a table horsing around with Minnie;

                    JUDY
          What'd ya' mean no coffy?

                    MINNIE
          I haven't had a chance to make it yet,
          Judy. I just finished preparing the
          stew.

                        JUDY
            Now Minnie, I'm not trying to tell you
            how to run your business. But I would
            think, coffy, would be the first thing
            you'd make.

The FOUR PASSENGERS
walk in. We only see their BOOTS enter Minnie's.

JUDY
sees the Passengers, hops off the table to her feet.

                        JUDY
            Come on in everybody, don't be shy.

Minnie takes one look at the four passengers, and says one
word;

                        MINNIE
            Hats!

The FOUR PASSENGERS
We see The Four Male Passengers. After Minnie yells at them,
they all four snatch off their cowboy hats. Three of the four
passengers are our old friends BOB, OSWALDO, and JOE GAGE.
The FOURTH PASSENGER it would appear is the leader of the
quartet.

                        JUDY
            Everybody, this is Minnie, and this
            is her place. Behind her pluckin' that
            chicken is Gemma.

Gemma smiles at The Four Passengers.

The Four Passengers walk further in towards Minnie.

                        JUDY
            Nice smile, that Gemma. Now the fella'
            in the uniform I don't know
                    (meaning General
                    Smithers)
            but the one he's playing chess with is
            Sweet Dave.
                    (to Sweet Dave)
            Hi ya' Dave!

Sweet Dave waves from his chair.

                        SWEET DAVE
            Hey Judy.

                        JUDY
            And Minnie, these are the passengers.

                    MINNIE
        Well that's not good enough. Take away
        them rags, let's see some faces, let's
        hear some names.

The Four Passengers lower the scarves that sit around their
faces, smiling at the friendly black woman.

                    OSWALDO
        Oswaldo Mobray, madame.

                    JOE GAGE
        Joe Gage.

                    BOB
        Bob.

                    THE FOURTH MAN
                    (smiling)
        And I'm Jody. It's a pleasant surprise
        to find such a warm sanctuary in the
        middle of such a cold hell.

                    MINNIE
        Well make yourself comfortable. Get
        warm by the fire.

                    JODY
        We're just gonna' go warm ourself's by
        the stove, if that's all right?

                    MINNIE
        Stove—fireplace—whatever. Just get
        warm.

                    JODY
        Oh, and Judy said something about the
        best coffy in the world. . . .?

                    OSWALDO
        Yes I do believe Judy did say something
        about the best coffy in the world.

                    MINNIE
        Well I don't know 'bout all that. But
        I'll tell ya' what it is. It's Hot and
        it's Strong, and it's Good. And in this
        snow it sure 'nuff warms your ass up.

                    JUDY
        You don't need to sell it, Minnie, you
        need to make it.

> MINNIE
> And you need to get your ass out there
> and help Charly with them bags. And get
> Ed in here.

> JUDY
> Yes, ma'am. But fix the coffy.

Judy bounces out.

> MINNIE
> (to Judy)
> I'll fix you!

The Four Passengers warm their hands by the pot belly stove,
and trade looks with one another.

EXT—MINNIE'S HABERDASHERY—MORNING

The two stagecoach drivers talking.

> JUDY
> I don't know. Some old man.

> ED
> Well I don't know what I'm suppose to do
> about it?

> JUDY
> I'm just tellin' you what she said.
> Anyway she sent me out here to help
> Charly. She wants to talk to you.

INT—MINNIE'S HABERDASHERY—MORNING

The FOUR PASSENGERS—SLOW MOTION
Check out the way station, as they warm their hands by the
pot belly stove.

JODY—SLOW MOTION
Checks out Minnie and Ed.

MINNIE and ED—SLOW MOTION
The black woman argues with the old white cowboy dude. As she
does, she ROLLS HER OWN SMOKE from a bag of Red Apple Tobacco.

BOB—SLOW MOTION
Watches the two old men play chess.

SWEET DAVE and GEN.SMITHERS—SLOW MOTION
Play chess.

OSWALDO—SLOW MOTION
Watches the young girl Gemma pluck the chicken.

GEMMA—SLOW MOTION
She plucks the chicken.

JOE GAGE—SLOW MOTION
Watches Judy and Charly unload the baggage on the stagecoach,
through the window.

JUDY and CHARLY—SLOW MOTION
Through the window unloading the bags from the stagecoach.

The Four Passengers are definitely staking the place out.

The Slow Motion kicks into twenty-four frames a second, and
we can hear the argument between Minnie and Ed.

                         MINNIE
                    (meaning Gen.Smithers)
               This Georgia cracker has been here
               three days, and I'm sick of it. I wanna
               'em ta' go to Red Rock. He wanna' go to
               Red Rock. Why can't you take 'em?

Ed points out the Four Passengers by the stove.

                         ED
               Look over there Minnie. You see 'em?
               Four Passengers. Two drivers. Ain't no
               seat.

                         MINNIE
               Three days of ole' white man stories.
               You hear what I'm sayin? Three goddamn
               days of OLD, WHITE, CRACKER, PECKAWOOD,
               HORSESHIT. I tell ya' Ed, I stood what I
               could stood, but I can't stand no mo'.

Minnie starts making her famous coffy as she nags the
stagecoach driver.

                         MINNIE
                    (CON'T)
               Naw naw naw, you need to take this
               motherfucker with you today. You feel
               that air out there don't 'cha? We might
               be gittin' a blizzard come tonight. I
               ain't sittin' holed up for three goddamn
               days with that ole' cracker.

We hear a LOUD SNAP and the death cry of a RAT OFF SCREEN.

                    MINNIE
                    (CON'T)
          I'll be good and dammed, that's another
          one of those little sonsabitches dead
          and gone!

Minnie's so happy about killing one of the basement rats,
she temporarily forgets about the Confederate General.

                    MINNIE
          Charly! You go down there and pick up
          that dead rat. I don't want him stinkin'
          up the place. Take Ceaser wit ya'.

Charly picks up a broom, and a TABBY CAT named CEASER. He
then walks over to a trap door in the floor that leads to
the basement. He puts the cat down on the floor. Ceaser the
cat is very excited. He knows what's in the basement. When
they let Ceaser hunt in the basement, those are the happiest
moments of Ceaser's feline life.

Charly lifts open the trap door in the floor.

Ceaser shoots down there like an arrow.

We hear the commotion under the floorboards of the rats
panicking and running away, and the cat chasing and killing
them.

After Ceaser's got the rodents' attention, Charly proceeds
downstairs into the basement, broom held fast.

Once he disappears in the floor, we hear him yelling at the
vermin;

                    CHARLY
          Git away you little bastards!
          You sonsabitches!

We hear the broom banging around.

The FOUR PASSENGERS
by the stove watch all this and trade looks. That's a very
interesting room down there. They also trade looks that say,
let's get this party started.

The Four Passengers, one at a time, take their positions.

JODY
starts the whole thing off. Moving from the pot belly stove
over to where Minnie is making coffy. She's smoking one of
her hand rolled cigarettes.

                    JODY
          Miss Minnie?

She turns towards him.

                    JODY
          Would you roll me a cigarette?

                    MINNIE
          Sure honey.

BOB
crosses the room over by the fireplace to watch the two old
men play chess. He just stands there watching their game.

They notice him.

Bob smiles at them and indicates for them to continue with
their game.

                    BOB
          Don't mind me gentlemen, I'm just
          watching.

                    SWEET DAVE
          You play?

                    BOB
          You know, I must of had at least twelve
          people teach me that goddamn game. Just
          never could keep the moves in my head.
          But if I'm not disturbing, I like to
          watch?

                    SWEET DAVE
          Hell no. I like whippin' this old man's
          ass in front of a audience.

                    GEN.SMITHERS
          You ain't whippin' shit.

JODY & MINNIE
Minnie hands Jody the cigarette she just rolled for him. Jody
accepts it with gallant flair.

                    JODY
          Merci beaucoup Mademoiselle Minnie.

Minnie giggles at being flirted to in French.

                    MINNIE
          Oh that's real nice! What is that?

                    JODY
          It's French.

                         MINNIE
          You speak French?

                         JODY
          Oui.

                         MINNIE
          Oui . . . . what does that mean?

                         JODY
          It means yes.

                         MINNIE
          Yes—Oui.
                    (to Sweet Dave)
          Hey Dave, ask me if my ass is fat.

                         SWEET DAVE
          What?

                         MINNIE
          Ask me if my ass is fat.

                         SWEET DAVE
          It is.

                         MINNIE
          I said ask me!

                         SWEET DAVE
          Why?

                         MINNIE
          Just do it!

                         SWEET DAVE
          Is your ass fat?

                         MINNIE
          Oui!
                    (to Jody)
          Look at that, I can speak French.

She giggles at herself, Minnie has a great giggle.

Jody lights the hand rolled smoke on a nearby candle, takes
a big drag, blows out a long stream of smoke, and says to
her;

                         JODY
          Delicious.

She playfully hits him (Minnie loves being flirted with).

OSWALDO
moves away from his position by the pot belly stove, over to
deeper in the kitchen area, where Gemma is plucking her chicken.

He indicates to her he's going to ask her a question.

She perks up to listen.

He asks with his most charming English accent;

                    OSWALDO
          Are you the jelly bean salesman around
          here?

He points at a large glass jar filled with multicolored jelly
beans high on the top shelf of a cabinet.

GEMMA
giggles and smiles, nodding her head, yes.

                    OSWALDO
          I'll take two bags. One for me, and one
          for . . . you.

                    GEMMA
          Really? You wanna' buy me jelly beans?

                    OSWALDO
          If I may be so bold.

The way he talks makes her giggle. Her pretty smile gets
even wider.

JOE GAGE
goes over to where the candy counter is. He opens up a glass
jar of green peppermint sticks.

                    JOE GAGE
                    (yells over
                    to Minnie)
          How many peppermint sticks a nickel buy me?

Minnie interrupts flirting with Jody.

                    MINNIE
                    (to Joe)
          Five.

Joe loudly slaps a nickel down on the counter. He removes
five green sticks, sticking one in his mouth, and putting
the other four in a little white bag.

Judy comes in carrying some of their luggage. Plopping it on
the floor.

                    JUDY
          I brought in your bags in case anybody wants
          to change your clothes before Red Rock.

She goes over to where Joe Gage is by the pot belly stove.
She warms her cold hands off the stove.

Handsome Joe Gage smiles at her.

Cute Judy smiles back.

He holds out the bag of candy and offers her a peppermint
stick.

                    JOE GAGE
          Peppermint stick?

                    JUDY
          Thanks.

She takes one and sticks it in her mouth.

Oswaldo Mobray watches Gemma move the ladder in place to
climb up and bring down the large jar of jelly beans.

Joe Gage sucks on his stick.

Judy sucks on hers.

                    JOE GAGE
          Why do they call you Six-Horse Judy?

                    JUDY
          Cause I'm the only Judy you've ever seen
          who could drive a six horse team.

                    JOE GAGE
          You gotta' accent there? Where you from,
          England?

Oswaldo chimes in from across the room.

                    OSWALDO
          I take exception to that!

Judy and Joe laugh.

                    JUDY
          New Zealand.

                    JOE GAGE
          Never heard of it. Is it anywhere by Old
          Zealand?

Judy flirts with the handsome bad boy.

The trap door in the floor opens up, and Ceaser (dead rat in his mouth) comes leaping out of the basement, followed closely by Charly carring a dead rat in his hand.

Oswaldo watches Gemma holding the large jar of jelly beans begin to climb down the ladder.

Minnie calls out;

                    MINNIE
        Coffy's ready!

                    ED
        It's about damn time.

Jody moves towards Ed and the coffy pot.

Ed sees Jody;

                    ED
                 (to Jody)
        Best coffy on the mountain.

Minnie smiles and waves away the compliment.

                    MINNIE
                 (to Jody)
        Stagecoach drivers like it. Passengers,
        not so much. Most find it a mite too
        strong.

She pours Ed a cup of coffy.

Bob watching the old men play chess, moves his hand by his gun butt.

Minnie pours Jody a cup of her coffy.

Oswaldo watching the pretty black gal struggling with the large jar of jelly beans, places his hand on his gun butt.

Jody takes a drink of Minnie's famous coffy.

Joe Gage quietly removes the pistol from the holster on the side of his hip. The cutie pie in the buckskins doesn't see this.

Ed, all smiles, and Minnie, all eyes, asks Jody;

                    MINNIE
        Well, what'd ya' think?

Jody answers by taking out his pistol and SHOOTING the surprised Minnie and Ed point blank.

Both Minnie and Ed hit the floor dead, her last pot of coffy still clutched in her hand, as she crashes to the floor.

Judy's head turns in the direction of the carnage.

Joe Gage raises his gun and FIRES into Judy's shoulder, blowing her across the room, and slamming her into a wood post.

Oswaldo removes his pistol from its holster and FIRES.

Shooting Gemma through the glass jar of jelly beans. She tumbles from the ladder to the floor.

Bob brings up his pistol and fanning the hammer SHOOTS Sweet Dave in his chair three times.

Judy shot in the shoulder, against the wood post. She looks across to Joe Gage with a complete lack of understanding, but a big question on her face.

He doesn't answer her questioning look, he just SHOOTS her a second time, this time more effectively. The bullet hits her square in the chest, wiping away her questioning expression, and spinning her hard to the floor.

Charly runs for the door.

Bob takes three WILD POT SHOTS at him, missing the boy, but hitting the lock on the front door.

Jody yells at Bob;

> JODY
> Christ almighty stop shootin' at that
> nigger fore ya' kill us all!

Bob stops.

> JODY
> (to Joe Gage)
> Grouch, finish 'em off.

EXT—MINNIE'S HABERDASHERY—MORNING

Charly runs out, trying to escape.

Joe Gage steps outside, and FIRES at Charly running away. The bullet hits Charly in the back, he plops down awkwardly in the snow.

INT—MINNIE'S HABERDASHERY—MORNING

Jody brings his pistol barrel against the temple
of Gen.Smithers, cocks back the hammer, and is just
ready to go bang, when suddenly Bob shouts at Jody in
SPANISH;

IN SPANISH SUBTITLED IN ENGLISH;

                    BOB
                    (SPANISH)
          Wait!

Jody stops.

                    BOB
                    (SPANISH)
          He's a nice touch.

                    JODY
                    (SPANISH)
          Him?

                    BOB
                    (SPANISH)
          He's authentic.

                    JODY
                    (SPANGLISH)
          We can't trust this
                    (ENGLISH)
          old fart.

                    BOB
                    (SPANISH)
          Sure we can. You just have to convince
          him to trust us.
                    (beat)
          Without those two fatsos, this place is
          going to seem real empty.
                    (switching to
                    ENGLISH to make
                    his point)
          He adds something.
          Not much. But something.

                    JODY
                    (to Oswaldo)
          What do you think, Pete?

Pete, it appears is OSWALDO.

                    OSWALDO
          I admit, he does make the setup more
          convincing.

                    JODY
          Okay, I'll talk to the old man. You and
          Grouch
                    (nickname for
                    Joe Gage)
          start getting rid of the bodies. Now
          don't try and bury nobody. Just stack
          'em on top of each other, and shovel
          some snow on top of 'em.

He goes over to the dead Sweet Dave, grabs him by his
sweater, and yanks him out of the chair onto the floor.

                    JODY
          Start with him.

As Joe and Oswaldo move to get Sweet Dave's body, Jody
instructs;

                    JODY
          Now stack 'em somewhere out back there.
          Just not by the two places where people go.
          The outhouse and the woodpile. Marco, . . .
                    (real name
                    of Bob)
          . . . start unhitching those horses and
          get 'em in the barn, and get 'em fed.
          When Ruth and Daisy get here, you're
          gonna' hafta' do it for them. After I
          get through with this ole' hickory tree
                    (meaning Gen.Smithers)
          I'll come help ya'.

Bob goes outside to work on the horses.

Oswaldo and Joe Gage carry out the dead bodies.

Jody looks down at The Old Man.

                    JODY
          Well old man, if you was a cat, what
          just happened here would count as one
          of your nine lives. You realize how
          close you came to being tossed on a
          pile of niggers?

                    GEN.SMITHERS
          Yes.

                    JODY
          And when it comes to that pile of
          niggers we building out back, won't take
          nothin' to make you General of it. You
          believe that?

GEN.SMITHERS
I expect no less.

JODY
Well not so fast old man. You might have
a way out yet.

Jody turns from the old man, and begins looking through
some of the trading post goods. Looking for and finding a
blanket. As he talks, he covers the blood stain on Sweet
Dave's chair with the blanket.

JODY
Later today, a dirty son of a gun's
gonna' come in here. He's gonna' have
my sister with him. He's gonna' have her
in chains. He's taking her into Red Rock
to be hung.

He finds a few other skins and pelts, and tosses them across
the chair as well.

JODY
You know why? Ten thousand dollars,
that's why.

Jody sits in Sweet Dave's chair, and continues explaining
his plan of action to the old officer.

JODY
(sits)
When he comes here I'm gonna' kill
that fella', and I'm gonna' let my
sister loose. Now do you have any
reason you'd want to interfere with
me saving my sister from a hangman's
rope?

GEN.SMITHERS
No.

JODY
You don't?

GEN.SMITHERS
No I don't.

JODY
Are you sure you don't? I mean we did
just kill Minnie and Sweet Dave. You
and Sweet Dave seemed pretty chummy
there.

> GEN.SMITHERS
> I just met those people. I'm here about
> my son. I don't give a damn about them,
> or you, or your sister, or any son of a
> bitch in Wyoming for that matter.

> JODY
> Good answer old man.
> (beat)
> So when they get here, you just sit
> your ass in this chair. And you don't
> do nothin', you don't say nothin'. Hello,
> thank you, good night—that's about it—
> Maybe your name—but that's it.

> GEN.SMITHERS
> Hello, thank you, good night, maybe my name.

> JODY
> Be an old man. Be dotty. Go to sleep.
> And don't say nothin'—and I mean
> nothin', to that bounty hunter got my
> sister. You understand?

> GEN.SMITHERS
> Yes.

> JODY
> Once it's safe, I kill him, free my
> sister, and leave you be.
> (holds out
> hand)
> Deal?

The old man shakes his hand.

> GEN.SMITHERS
> Deal.

Jody the outlaw leader takes his hand away from the old man,
and looks across at the General suspiciously.

> JODY
> Now you ain't playin' foxy grandpa with
> me now, are you?

> GEN.SMITHERS
> No.

> JODY
> I don't have a trusting nature, old man.
> (beat)
> But we'll give it a try.

He pats the old man's knee, and stands up.

EXT—MINNIE'S HABERDASHERY—MORNING

Joe Gage comes pushing a wheelbarrow with a dead Minnie in it. Followed by Oswaldo and Jody carrying the dead body of Gemma.

Bob is in the B.G. unhitching the horses from the stagecoach.

Joe pushes the wheelbarrow behind the Haberdashery...finally finding a spot out back where lies the dead body of Sweet Dave. Joe dumps Minnie out next to him.

MINNIE'S DEAD BODY
is dumped on the snowy ground next to the dead Sweet Dave. We hold for a beat or two on her dead body, when the dead Gemma is thrown on top of her.

BOB
unhitches horses from the stagecoach.

OSWALDO AND JOE
carry the dead Judy to the pile.

BOB
leads a horse into the stable.

OSWALDO AND JOE
toss Judy on the pile of bodies.

DEAD JUDY
lies on the ground.

JOE SHOVELS
snow.

BOB
feeds one of the horses.

OSWALDO SHOVELS
snow.

DEAD JUDY
gets snow shoveled on her.

JOE SHOVELING
snow.

DEAD ED
gets snow shoveled on him.

The two men next to the pile of six bodies covered in snow.

INT—MINNIE'S HABERDASHERY—DAY
Jody climbs up top through the door in the floor, and joins
Bob in the kitchen area.

                    JODY
                 (to Bob)
        Other than those damn blasted rats
        down there, that basement's perfect. I
        can sit right underneath that dirty so
        an' so's nose the entire time, and Ruth
        won't be the wiser.

                    BOB
        Unless he checks the basement.

                    JODY
        Shitfire I hope he does. I'll shoot 'em
        dead climbin' down that ladder. End of
        story, end of problem.

Jody rips pieces of cloth off of an old rag, and sticks it in
both ears.

                    BOB
        How many rats down there?

                    JODY
        I dunno' . . . a few?

                    BOB
        You gonna' be down there all night with
        a bunch of rats?

                    JODY
        A room fulla' rabbits ain't gonna' stop
        me from savin' my sister. Specially
        after I go down there and show them
        bunny's who's boss.

He picks up the lantern, opens the trap door in the floor,
and descends into the basement.

WE HEAR UP TOP Jody go down there and start both YELLING
and SHOOTING at the rats. He empties both pistols at the
scurrying rodents.

Oswaldo and Joe Gage come back inside, hearing all the
shooting going on underneath the floor.

                    OSWALDO
        What's with all the shooting?

Jody walks to the trap door, and says up to them;

>   JODY
>   Just demonstrating the new basement
>   rules to these rats.

>   JOE
>   How's that goin'?

>   JODY
>   They get the general idea.
>   (beat)
>   Can you believe this room, it's perfect.

He sees the worried looks on both of their faces.

>   JODY
>   (CON'T)
>   What's wrong?

>   OSWALDO
>   Bad news.

EXT—SNOWY MOUNTAIN TOP—MORNING

Oswaldo, Joe Gage, Bob, and Jody take a hike to a mountain
top clearing, and look down off the cliff to see what's
coming at them.

What they see is bad weather.

>   JODY
>   What's that?

>   OSWALDO
>   Having lived in Switzerland, I can
>   tell you exactly what that is. It's a
>   blizzard.

>   JODY
>   A blizzard? Is it gonna' hit us for
>   sure?

>   OSWALDO
>   Oh yes.

>   JODY
>   When?

>   OSWALDO
>   Sometime tonight.

                    BOB
          If there's a blizzard coming we can't
          stay in that shack.

                    JODY
          Get some gumption, Marco. That shack
          probably sees about twelve blizzards a
          year. If we hadn't killed Minnie and her
          nigger menagerie, what would they do?
          They'd hole up, that's what they'd do.

                    OSWALDO
          I'm afraid I have to agree with mi amigo
          here. We should move on to Red Rock
          while we have the chance.

                    JODY
          If them niggers can ride it out at
          Minnie's, so can we. We ain't movin' no
          damn where, we're holin' up.

Bob (aka "MARCO") makes an exasperated noise.

Jody turns to him;

                    JODY
          You got something you wanna' say?

                    BOB
          Have you ever been in a blizzard?

                    JODY
          No.

                    BOB
          I didn't think so. Funny how the people
          who have been in a blizzard are the
          ones who want to go. And the people who
          don't know what the hell they're talking
          about, are the ones who want to stay.

                    JODY
          Look, John Ruth is a rattlesnake. And the
          only way we're gonna' separate him from
          my sister is catch him off guard or at
          least on awkward footing. Now before they
          get to Red Rock, him here with a spoon in
          his mouth seemed the best bet.
          But if he has to sit here on his ass for
          three days chained to Daisy, waiting
          for the sun to come out . . . at some
          point . . . he's gotta' close his eyes.
          And that's when you blow the top of his
          head off.

                    JOE GAGE
          Look ambushing John Ruth while he ate
          was always risky for Daisy. But it was
          the best chance we had, so we were
          gonna' chance it.
          This blizzard changes everything.
          And if the idea is to safely separate
          Daisy from this joker, this sit-tight-
          during-the-blizzard idea is obviously
          the safest way for Daisy.

                    JODY
          Well if that's obviously the safest way
          to free Daisy, that's obviously the way
          we're gonna' do it. Daisy ain't just
          my sister. She's a goddamn dependable
          member of this gang. And if any one of
          you ain't willin' to brave a blizzard to
          save a member of your own gang from a
          rope, you ought' not be ridin' with 'em.

I guess they heard that.

INT—MINNIE'S HABERDASHERY—SNOWY DAY

Grouch Douglass tosses a table on top of another table
face down.

English Pete does the same thing.

Both men hammer a nail into the underside of the table.

FROM THE FRONT WINDOW OF MINNIE'S
We see O.B. and Ruth's chartered stagecoach arrive.

MARCO
watches too.

                    MARCO
                  (Spanish)
          Here they come.

Grouch takes the hammer and hits the pounded in nail on the
side, turning it into a hook.

JODY
Grabs a BIG BEAR SKIN, wrapping it around his shoulders, he
says to his men;

                    JODY
          Okay boys, this is it, get ready!

English Pete bends his nail into a hook.

Grouch turns the table back on its legs. Then takes one of his pistols and hangs it underneath the table on the self made hook.

Marco piles on his winter wear.

English Pete hangs his pistol on an under the table nail/ hook.

Jody goes to the cellar door, throws it open, and tells his men;

> JODY
> Now remember, it doesn't matter if we
> have four men or forty, we're still
> gonna' be facing John Ruth chained to
> my sister with a pistol pointed at her
> belly. Now killin' that fella' 'fore he
> kills my sister, ain't gonna' be easy.
> But you best believe that's exactly what
> we're gonna' do. So the name of the game
> here is patience. Trapped here for two
> or three days, at some point, he will
> close his eyes.

> GROUCH
> I think the first forty-five seconds
> he's in the room is a good time.

> JODY
> If you gotta' shot Grouch, you take it.
> But be right.

Jody disappears in the cellar, closing the door in the floor behind him, but before he does he yells to the seated General Smithers;

> JODY
> (yelling)
> Remember old man, my sister don't leave
> this mountain alive, neither do you!

> GEN.SMITHERS
> (yells back)
> I'll do my best!

The rest of the gang, Grouch, English Pete, and Marco the Mexican walk towards the front door. Marco is all bundled up. All three men look at each other. This is it. Good luck amigos. They pry open the door and Marco exits to deal with the stagecoach. Pete and Grouch nail the door shut.

SMASH CUT TO

INT—MINNIE'S HABERDASHERY—DAY

TIME CUT: MINUTES LATER

JOHN RUTH KICKS OPEN THE DOOR (the front door of Minnie's), YANKING DOMERGUE in behind him, he SLAMS the door, only to see it doesn't have a lock.

We now show the audience this scene again, except this time from the perspective of The Domergue Gang, Grouch Douglass (Joe Gage), English Pete Hicox (Oswaldo Mobray) and Daisy Domergue.

After seeing MARCO THE MEXICAN (BOB) outside, Domergue sees her two favorite gang members inside, GROUCH DOUGLASS (JOE GAGE) and ENGLISH PETE HICOX (OSWALDO MOBRAY).

GROUCH DOUGLASS   &   ENGLISH PETE HICOX
(JOE GAGE)   (OSWALDO MOBRAY)
Sitting at his table.   Sitting in Sweet Dave's chair.

                    GROUCH (JOE) & ENGLISH PETE (OSWALDO)
               You have to nail it shut!

DOMERGUE & JOHN RUTH
look at them, "What?"

                    GROUCH (JOE) & ENGLISH PETE (OSWALDO)
               There's hammer and nails by the door!

John Ruth turns to hold the door closed, sees the can of nails by his feet and the hammer lying beside it.

He indicates for Domergue to hold the door closed. She does.

John Ruth BANGS the nail with the hammer.

ENGLISH PETE, sitting in Sweet Dave's chair, watches the bounty hunter pound the nail. Then shifts his eyes over to Gen.Smithers, who looks down at his lap.

                    ENGLISH PETE (OSWALDO)
                    (whispering)
               Look at me old man.

The Old Man brings his eyes up to the Englishman across from him.

                    ENGLISH PETE (OSWALDO)
               Easy old boy. One wrong gesture...one
               awkwardly worded sentence...I put a
               bullet in your gizzard.

The BANGING stops.

Grouch (Joe) yells;

> GROUCH (JOE)
> You need to do...

English Pete joins in...

> GROUCH & ENGLISH PETE
> ...two pieces of wood!

Both Domergue and John Ruth give them a bit of "a look", then turn back to the door and get to work.

BANG BANG BANG goes the hammer.

GROUCH DOUGLASS (JOE GAGE) sits at his table with his diary and writing utensils in front of him.

The CAMERA PANS DOWN BELOW THE TABLE. We see Grouch fingering the pistol in his holster with his gun hand.

John Ruth finishes hammering in the second piece of wood.

> JOHN RUTH
> That door's a son of a gun. Who's the idiot
> that broke that, that Mexican fella'?

Him and Domergue turn to face the room.

DOMERGUE sees ENGLISH PETE, who hops to his feet.

> ENGLISH PETE (OSWALDO)
> Good heavens, a woman out in this white
> hell.

Domergue smiles at Pete's foppish accent.

> ENGLISH PETE (OSWALDO)
> (to Domergue)
> You must be frozen solid, poor thing.

> JOHN RUTH
> (to Oswaldo)
> Where's the coffy?

English Pete points to the pot belly stove and the non deadly BLUE COFFY POT. John Ruth YANKS Domergue over to it.

ENGLISH PETE
as OSWALDO MOBRAY hurries over to where John Ruth is making
coffy, and makes conversation. But his real purpose is to
cut off John Ruth, and make the bounty hunter STOP and pay
attention to the little English man. Which is another way of
saying, not paying attention to Grouch Douglass, whose plan
is to shoot John Ruth from his chair, if he can get a good
shot, during the bounty hunter's first disorienting sixty
seconds in the room.

                    JOHN RUTH
          Looks like Minnie's got 'er a full
          house. When did you fella's arrive?

                    ENGLISH PETE (OSWALDO)
          About forty minutes ago.

UNDERNEATH GROUCH'S TABLE
His gun hand removes his pistol from its holster. The end of
the barrel finds John Ruth.

John Ruth turns and gestures towards Grouch at the table.
English Pete steps into Ruth's line of vision ever so
slightly blocking his view.

                    JOHN RUTH
          Is that your driver?

                    ENGLISH PETE (OSWALDO)
          No, he's a passenger. The driver
          lit out. He said he was going to
          spend the blizzard shacked up
          with a friend.

John Ruth was more concentrated on pouring his coffy than
listening to English Pete's horse shit story.

                    JOHN RUTH
          Lucky devil.

John Ruth takes a drink of coffy and spits it out.

                    JOHN RUTH
          Jesus Christ, that's awful!

ENGLISH PETE & DOMERGUE
laugh.

                    JOHN RUTH
          Christ almighty, what that Mexican
          fella' do, soak his ole' socks in
          the pot?

UNDERNEATH GROUCH'S TABLE
His thumb COCKS BACK the pistol's hammer.

CAMERA BEHIND PISTOL
He moves the pistol barrel to get the best shot of John Ruth.

> ENGLISH PETE (OSWALDO)
> I think we all felt the same way,
> but were a little too polite to say
> something.

> DOMERGUE
> He don't have that problem.

> JOHN RUTH
> Where's the coffy?

> ENGLISH PETE (OSWALDO)
> There.

John Ruth starts making coffy.

Giving Grouch Douglass a perfect target of his broad back.

> JOHN RUTH
> So all three of you on the way to Red
> Rock when the blizzard stopped ya', huh?

English Pete catches Domergue's eye.

With his hand held low, he gestures with his fingers for her
to step away from John Ruth (as much as she can).

> ENGLISH PETE (OSWALDO)
> Yes, all three of us were on that
> stagecoach out there.

Domergue sees the gesture, and looks to Pete's eyes.

> JOHN RUTH
> Where's the well water?

> ENGLISH PETE (OSWALDO)
> Right there.

Domergue's eyes shift over to Grouch, and she sees the
pistol pointed at John Ruth.

Daisy BLURTS OUT;

> DOMERGUE
> The new Sheriff of Red Rock is
> traveling with us.

English Pete's eyebrows instinctively raise.

Grouch changes his mind about shooting John Ruth.

> JOHN RUTH
> Sheriff of Red Rock, that'll be the
> day! If he's a goddamn sheriff, I'm a
> monkey's uncle.

> DOMERGUE
> Good, then you can share bananas with
> your nigger friend in the stable.

Both English Pete and Grouch Douglass hear this.

UNDERNEATH GROUCH'S TABLE
The pistol is replaced in its holster.

> GROUCH
> (to himself)
> Look's like we're gonna' hafta' do this
> the hard way.

Pete, hearing "nigger friend in the stable", but ignoring it,
asks;

> ENGLISH PETE (OSWALDO)
> So the new Sheriff of Red Rock is
> traveling with you?

> JOHN RUTH
> He's lyin', he ain't sheriff of nothin'.
> He's a southern renegade. He's just
> talkin' his self outta' freezin' to
> death, is all.

                                    CUT TO

INT—MINNIE'S BASEMENT—UNDERGROUND

Jody Domergue listening to what's being said in the room
above him.

As John Ruth talks brutal to his sister, a nasty sneer
breaks out on Jody's mouth.

> JOHN RUTH (OS)
> (to Domergue)
> What the fuck I tell you 'bout talkin'?
> I will bust you in the mouth right in
> front of these people, I don't give a
> fuck!

                    JODY
                    (quietly to
                    himself)
          I'll remember you said that to my
          sister, when I cut off all your fingers
          and make you eat them one by one.

                                        CUT TO BLACK

Last Chapter

BLACK MAN, White HELL

WE FOLLOW
Chris' bleeding leg, using a chair as a crutch, leaving a
blood trail behind him, as he reaches the side of Minnie and
Sweet Dave's bed. Maj.Warren, holding his bloody crotch where
his balls used to be, lies in the bed.

He's holding John Ruth's pistol-rifle.

Both Maj.Warren and Cap't.Mannix have shed their uniform
jackets. Both men are sweating on the outside and burning up
on the inside.

Chris sits in the chair by the bed, and talks to
Maj.Warren.

                    CHRIS
          How ya' doin' oleboy?

                    MAJ.WARREN
          I got my nuts blown off, I'm bleedin'
          like a stuck pig, I'm gonna' die, and
          these motherfuckers did it, that's how
          I'm doin'. How you doin'?

                    CHRIS
          Well my leg hurts really bad, but I
          think—

                    MAJ.WARREN
          I was bein' sarcastic, I don't give a
          fuck about your leg!

                    CHRIS
          Just make yourself comfortable.

                    MAJ.WARREN
          Don't worry about my comfort, I can't
          feel my ass no more. Worry about these
          owl hoots and that bushwackin' nut
          shooter in the basement.

Chris starts negotiating with the fella' in the basement.

                    CHRIS
          Alright...you...fella' in the
          basement. You either give up by the
          time I count to three...or...I shoot
          Domergue in the head.

Chris on one side of the bed, points the rifle in Domergue's
direction.

Warren points his pistol at Domergue.

                         CHRIS
          One! . . . . . Two! . . . . .

                         JODY (OS)
          Don't shoot her in the head! I'm comin'
          up!

                         MAJ.WARREN
          Not so fast bushwacking nut shooter . . .
          first open the door . . . but you don't
          come out till we tell you come out.

The door OPENS.

But Jody keeps duck down in the basement.

                         CHRIS
          Now throw out your pistols!

A single PISTOL flies up out of the basement, landing with a
CLUNK on the hard wood floor.

                         CHRIS
          Now the other one!

                         JODY (OS)
          I only have one!

                         MAJ.WARREN
          Well then you better shit a pistol
          outta' your ass, cause if you don't
          throw another one up here in the next
          two seconds, this bitch is gonna' die!

Beat.

Then a second PISTOL plops up out of the basement and onto
the hard wood floor with a THUD.

                         CHRIS
          Now, with your hands where we can see
          'em, slowly come on up!

Jody starts to climb out of the basement . . . slowly . . . . he
emerges from the hole in the floor.

Like Winnie the Pooh, he's half in—half out.

He looks to Maj.Warren and Chris with their guns on the bed.
Then turns around and sees his sister on the floor. Their
eyes meet.

                        JODY
            How you doin' dummy?

                        DOMERGUE
                        (gives a toothless
                        smile)
            Better now I see your ugly face.

Jody smiles...

WHEN
Maj.Warren shoots him in the back of the head...
His scalp flies off...

CU DOMERGUE
His blood and brains SPLASH her in the face.

She screams!

Jody's body disappears in the basement.

Maj.Warren yells after it;

                        MAJ.WARREN
            How do you like that one, bushwacking
            nutshooter?

                        DOMERGUE
            You fucking bastard! He was giving up!

                        MAJ.WARREN
            Wrong bitch, he gave up.

He turns his attention to Joe Gage against the back wall.

                        MAJ.WARREN
            Joe Gage, shut that door.

Joe Gage walks from the back wall, looks in the hole, and
shuts the basement door.

                        DOMERGUE
            Is he dead?

Joe turns to her.

                        JOE GAGE
            Yeah.
                        (pause)
            Sorry, honey.
                        (He turns to
                        Maj.Warren)
            Can I sit in a chair?

                    MAJ.WARREN
        Yeah.

Joe Gage sits in the chair at the table across from the bed
and next to Daisy.

We CUT to
underneath the table. The huge HOG LEG that Grouch Douglass
stashed there in Chapter Five hangs by a nail under the
table. We see Joe Gage's legs enter under the table.

                    DOMERGUE
        Mannix, you sure picked the wrong time
        to turn into a nigger lover!
        Don't you see that nigger and John Ruth
        put you smack dab in the middle of
        danger? You're about to be murdered in
        some nigger named Minnie's house and
        you don't even know why!

                    CHRIS
        Okay bitch, I'll bite . . . why?

                    DOMERGUE
        I am workin' with all three of them
        fella's . . . but not because they got
        butterflies in their belly 'bout me.
        We're all gang members. THE JODY
        DOMERGUE GANG. That fella' you just
        killed in the basement was Jody
        Domergue.

                    MAJ.WARREN
        Last I heard about The Domergue Gang,
        they were deep in Mexico, around
        Chihuahua? What'd bring 'em out this way?

                    DOMERGUE
        Me. I'm Jody's sister.

                    CHRIS
        Then how come y'all have different
        names?

                    DOMERGUE
        We don't, idiot!

                    CHRIS
        Who the hell is Jody Doe-ming-grey?

                    DOMERGUE
        Wanna' tell 'em bounty man?

>   MAJ.WARREN
>   (to Chris)
> He's a big bad cat. He's worth fifty
> thousand dollars, and every member of
> his gang is worth at least ten.
>   (to Domergue)
> Which finally explains why you're worth
> ten.

>   DOMERGUE
>   (to Maj.Warren)
> And what's gonna' happen when that sun
> comes out nigger, so is my brother's
> fifteen men—comin' straight here
> for us!
>   (to Joe)
> Tell 'em Grouch!

>   JOE(GROUCH)
> Jody's got fifteen men waitin' in Red
> Rock. If we weren't able to kill John
> Ruth and free Daisy here, it's their job
> to sack the town, kill John Ruth and
> free Daisy there.
>   (to Chris)
> But the point is Chris, you ain't part
> of this drama. We are, Warren is, Ruth
> was, but you ain't. So...let's make a
> deal?

>   CHRIS
>   (to Domergue)
> You're gonna' make a deal with me? I
> just shot Oswaldo.

>   DOMERGUE
> Yeah, but he shot you too, and he shot
> you first. And that was before you
> knew the situation, but now you know
> the situation. Look, this only works if
> we're all reasonable.
>   (to Oswaldo)
> Pete, tell 'em no hard feelin's?

>   OSWALDO
>   (coughs blood)
> No worries, mate.

>   DOMERGUE
> Now with my brother dead, I'm in charge
> of this gang. Right boys?

                    JOE GAGE / OSWALDO
          That's right, Daisy!

                    DOMERGUE
          And Chris I'm tellin' you, you ain't
          done anything yet, we can't forgive.
          So...let's make a deal?

The SWEATY, and NOW TREMBLING Maj.Warren COCKS BACK the
hammer on his pistol....

                    MAJ.WARREN
                    (to Domergue)
          No deals, tramp!

Jackrabbit quick, she spits to Chris;

                    DOMERGUE
          You gonna' let that nigger speak for
          you Chris?

Maj.Warren starts to point the pistol in Daisy's direction.

When Chris turns to him and calls out;

                    CHRIS
          Hold it Warren!
          Seein' as she ain't got nothin' to sell,
          I'm kinda curious about her sales pitch.
          Humor me.
                    (to Domergue)
          Alright bitch, what's your deal?

                    DOMERGUE
          Easy. Take your gun and shoot that
          nigger dead. Then we sit here all nice
          like for the next two days. When the
          snow melts, we go to Mexico, and you go
          on to Red Rock to get that star pinned
          on your chest.
                    (to Oswaldo)
          Hey Pete, how much can we pay him?

Oswaldo (English Pete), dying in Sweet Dave's Chair, drops
his foppish accent and says;

                    OSWALDO (ENGLISH PETE)
                    (to Domergue)
          Well, we can give 'em Marco.
                    (to Chris)
          Bob's real name is "Marco The Mexican".
          He's worth twelve thousand dollars.

                        MAJ.WARREN
                        (to Oswaldo)
            That's "Marco The Mexican"?

                        OSWALDO (ENGLISH PETE)
            Precisely.

                        MAJ.WARREN
            Well, after I blew his face off, Marco
            ain't worth a peso.

                        OSWALDO (ENGLISH PETE)
            Well then...if I die in the next two
            days, which is more than likely, you
            can have me. Under the name ENGLISH
            PETE HICOX I've gotta' fifteen thousand
            dollar federal bounty on my head.
                        (he points at Chris
                        with a finger from a
                        bloody red hand)
            And it's all yours Chris.

Maj.Warren threatens English Pete with his gun.

                        MAJ.WARREN
            Keep talkin' Pete, you gonna' talk
            yourself to death.
                        (he shifts his eyes
                        over to Joe Gage)
            Who you be, Joe Gage?

                        JOE GAGE
            GROUCH DOUGLASS.

                        CHRIS
                        (to Maj.Warren)
            You know 'em?

                        MAJ.WARREN
                        (to Chris)
            Yeah, I know of Grouch Douglass. He's
            worth ten thousand, just like Domergue.

                        CHRIS
                        (to Domergue)
            Remind me why wouldn't we just kill all
            y'all and cash in?

Domergue reminds him.

                    DOMERGUE
                 (to Chris)
          Oh, you can kill us all. But you'll
          never spend a cent of that bounty
          money. And you'll never leave this
          mountain alive.
                 (beat)
          Because when that snow melts, the rest of
          Jody's gang—all fifteen of 'em—that were
          waiting in Red Rock are comin' here.
                 (changing tone)
          Now let's say you shoot us all. If you
          want all that Domergue Gang bounty
          money, you still got to get all our
          corpses into Red Rock. And that ain't
          gonna' be so easy. Cause I doubt you can
          drive a four horse team. And that wagon
          out there is too heavy for a two horse
          team. So that means you're gonna'
          hafta' lead a string of horses into Red
          Rock. And with that deep snow after a
          blizzard, you ain't gonna' be able to
          get away with any more then one body per
          horse. So that's YOU, leading a string
          of FOUR horses into Red Rock.
          And with all them horses, in that snow,
          and you all by your lonesome . . . you're
          gonna' be a mite poky.
          And you're gonna' run smack dab into
          The Domergue Gang.
                 (to Grouch)
          And again Grouch, how many is that?

                    GROUCH DOUGLASS
          Fifteen killers strong.

                    DOMERGUE
          And when those fifteen killers come
          across <u>you</u>, in possession of all of our
          dead bodies, they ain't just gonna' kill
          you and that nigger. They're gonna'
          go back to Red Rock and kill every
          son-of-a-bitch in that town.
          You really the Sheriff of Red Rock?
          You wanna' save the town?
          Then shoot that nigger dead!

Maj.Warren on the big iron bed FIRES his pistol.

Domergue's FOOT IS ALMOST BLOWN OFF by Maj.Warren's pistol.

Not because Maj.Warren was trying to shoot her in the foot.
When he pulled the trigger he was positive it was a head
shot. He's trembling so badly he can barely hold the pistol.

DOMERGUE'S SCREAMS
fill the rafters!

                    DOMERGUE
            Jesus Christ!

                    MAJ.WARREN
            Oh, you believe in Jesus now, huh bitch?
            Good, cause you gonna' meet 'em.

The SWEATING AND TREMBLING MAJ.WARREN turns his pistol on
the whole room, and says; "Anybody else wanna' make a deal?"

ENGLISH PETE HICOX (OSWALDO)
dying in Sweet Dave's Chair, looks at the bloody Daisy on
the floor. Then takes a glance at his old friend Grouch
Douglass standing against the wall at the mercy of Warren's
and Chris' pistols. Knowing he ain't living through no
blizzard, English Pete makes a move for his old friends. He
coughs up a little more blood into the handkerchief, raises
up a bloody finger, and says up to Chris;

                    ENGLISH PETE (OSWALDO)
            Deal still goes Chris. You didn't do
            anything we can't forgive. It's still all on
            that nigger. Shoot 'em dead, take my body,
            and sit out the snow with Daisy and Grou—

MAJ.WARREN BLOWS ENGLISH PETE OUTTA' his chair with his
pistol.

UNDER THE TABLE
Grouch grabs the gun.

Joe Gage stands up holding his HOG LEG and FIRES A BLAST
towards the bed.

It HITS THE PILLOW EXPLODING IT.

Maj.Warren FIRES his pistol, hitting Joe Gage spinning him
around...

Chris FIRES his pistol-rifle, hitting Joe and spinning him
around...

Chris Mannix FIRES his pistol-rifle again, hitting Joe Gage
spinning him around to the other end of the room.

Joe Gage hits the floor and dies.

Maj.Warren turns his pistol on Domergue...He cocks back the hammer.

She closes her eyes.

CLICK.

His gun is empty.

Everybody looks at everybody realizing the situation from their own selfish point of view.

Chris says to Domergue, as if they hadn't stopped talking;

> CHRIS
> So we sit here all nice and friendly like for the next two days, then the snow melts, and you leave here, meet up with your gang, and high tail it to Mexico? That's the deal, right?

> DOMERGUE
> Yeah.

> CHRIS
> And I get Oswaldo and Joe Gage?

> DOMERGUE
> Yeah.

> CHRIS
> Jody's worth fifty thousand, what about his body?

> MAJ.WARREN
> You're gonna' make a deal with that diabolical bitch?

> CHRIS
> I'm not sayin' I'm gonna' make a deal with her. We're just talkin'. Calm down.
> (to Domergue)
> So what about Jody's body and the fifty thousand?

> DOMERGUE
> You're getting greedy Reb. No deal. We're takin' Jody's body back with us. He's got children.

> CHRIS
> So I kill Warren and we're all friends?

                    DOMERGUE
          Yeah.

Chris thinks about it, and says;

                    CHRIS
          No deal tramp.

                    DOMERGUE
          Chris, you're makin' the biggest mistake
          of your life! When our boys get here in
          a coupla' days, they're gonna' cut your
          nuts off. And there won't be a stick
          left in that town unburnt.

Both Chris and Warren are losing a lot of blood.

A big pool of blood from Chris' leg sits at his feet under
his chair.

The bed is soaked in blood, and dripping into a pool on the
floor.

Chris painfully stands up from the chair.

                    CHRIS
          Well I guess I should be plum scared
          right now, huh?

                    DOMERGUE
          If you had any brains, you would be.

                    CHRIS
          You see, here's the problem, Daisy.
          In order for me to be scared of your
          threats, I gotta' believe in those
          fifteen extra gang members waitin' it
          out in Red Rock.
          And boy oh boy I sure don't.
          What I believe is, Joe Gage or Grouch
          Douglass or whatever the fuck his name
          was, poisoned the coffy, and you watched
          him do it.
          And you watched me pour a cup, and you
          didn't say shit.
          And...I believe you are what you've
          always been, a lyin' bitch who will do
          anything to cheat that rope waitin' for
          you in Red Rock. Including shittin' out
          fifteen extra gang members whenever she
          needs be.

Using the chair as a crutch he moves away from the bed, more
in her direction.

                    CHRIS
          And I believe, when it comes to what's
          left of the Jody Doe-ming-grey Gang, I'm
          lookin' at 'em right now dead on this
          mothrfuckin' floor.

                    DOMERGUE
          Then you're gonna' die on this
          mountain, Chris. Because my brother
          leads an army of men.

                    CHRIS
          Horse Shit! My daddy led an army, he led
          a renegade army fightin' a lost cause!
          He held up to four hundred men together
          after the war with nothing but their
          respect in his command. Your brother's
          just an owl hoot who led a gang of
          killers.

Then the loss of blood, and the physical exertion, finally
catches up with Chris.

His eyes flutter and he says;

                    CHRIS
          I don't feel so good.

Mannix passes out, hitting the floor hard.

She moves towards the gun, the chain holding her wrist to
John Ruth, stops her.

Maj.Warren in bed, yells to Chris;

                    MAJ.WARREN
          You still alive, boy?

Domergue DRAGS John's body to a shelf. On that shelf she
picks up a hatchet, and starts HACKING John Ruth's ARM OFF.

Maj.Warren in the bed watches this and yells to Chris;

                    MAJ.WARREN
          Unless your goddamn ass is nailed to
          the floor, you better wake the fuck up!

Domergue has almost CHOPPED THROUGH the arm.

Chris EYES FLUTTER....he's starting to come to.

Domergue, after HACKING AWAY at the arm with a hatchet, gives it A FEW GOOD YANKS. The arm is TORN AWAY from John Ruth's body, John's arm still in the manacle, still chained to Domergue's wrist.

Domergue is FREE!

Maj.Warren screams from his bed;

>   MAJ.WARREN
>   Wake up, white boy!

She rises to her feet.

Her EYES go to Chris' pistol.

Chris shakes the pain out of his head.

Domergue makes a RUNNING GRAB/DIVE for the Pistol.

Chris' arm comes out of frame, picking up the gun, and FIRES HITTING Domergue in the shoulder, BLOWING her across the floor.

>   CHRIS
>   (to Maj.Warren)
>   I ain't dead yet, you black bastard.

Maj.Warren breaks out in a hardy Spaghetti Western gallows laugh.

>   MAJ.WARREN
>   You know Chris, I may have misjudged
>   you.

Chris with his pistol barrel in Domergue's face.

>   CHRIS
>   This one did, that's for damn sure.
>   (to Domergue)
>   Now we come to the part of the story
>   where I blow your head off.

Maj.Warren YELLS from the bed;

>   MAJ.WARREN
>   Don't shoot her, Mannix!

>   CHRIS
>   Why the hell not?

                    MAJ.WARREN
        John Ruth might of been one mighty
        mighty bastard. But the best thing that
        bastard did 'fore he died was save your
        life.
                    (beat)
        We're gonna' die, white boy. And we
        ain't got no say in that. But there's
        one thing left we do have a say in.
        How we kill this bitch. And I "say",
        shootin's too good for her. If John Ruth
        wanted to shoot her, he coulda' shot
        her anytime anywhere along the way. But
        John Ruth was "The Hangman". And when
        The Hangman catches ya', you don't die
        by a bullet, when The Hangman catches
        ya', you hang.

Chris starts to catch Maj.Warren's drift.

                    CHRIS
                    (remembering)
        "You only need to hang Mean Bastards.
        But Mean Bastards, <u>you</u> <u>need</u> <u>to</u> <u>hang</u>".

                                            CUT TO

A HANGMAN'S NOOSE is put around Domergue's neck.

Chris throws the rope over the ceiling beam, it makes him cringe.

Chris leaning against the bed, with Maj.Warren's help, HOISTS THE ROPE . . .

PULLING ON DOMERGUE'S NECK and lifting her feet off the ground.

Domergue KICKS HER FEET.

Chris and Maj.Warren YANK HARD on the rope, SCREAMING!

Domergue is YANKED WAY UP. She hangs by the neck, suffocating, while John Ruth's wrist hangs off of her chain.

DOMERGUE'S FACE
as the rope cuts in.

CHRIS SCREAMS!

> CHRIS
> As my first and final act as the Sheriff
> of Red Rock, I sentence you, Domergue,
> to hang by the neck until dead.

He YANKS the rope again.

She goes higher.

As she twists and turns, Chris ties off the rope and collapses on the floor.

Until she fights and kicks herself out, and is just hanging from the rope dead.

Chris on the floor by the bed, and Maj.Warren on the bed look up and watch her die.

After she dies, Chris looks up at Maj.Warren;

> CHRIS
> Hey, can I see that Lincoln Letter?

> MAJ.WARREN
> Sure.

Maj.Warren reaches his bloody hand into his jacket, and pulls out the letter, smearing red blood all over the white envelope. He hands it to Chris, who with dripping red blood hands of his own, takes the envelope, opens it up, and takes out the letter, smearing blood all over it.

Chris reads it, as the WIND BLOWS inside, Domergue SWINGS from the rope.

Just then, CEASER The CAT, who must've been hiding all this time, finally decides the anxiety in Minnie's has calmed down considerably, and jumps up on the bed, joining the two men.

He's hungry, and makes a hungry sound to the fella's.

Maj.Warren looks over at the cat.

>   MAJ.WARREN
>   Where did you come from?

Chris reads.

>   CHRIS
>   "Ole' Mary Todd". That's a nice touch.

>   MAJ.WARREN
>   Thanks.

                                        CUT TO BLACK

                           THE END